FLIGHT OR FOLLY?

He took his feet out of the stirrups, gave himself a little push and floated into the air. He moved his arms and legs experimentally and rocked erratically. He tried to scramble back for the stirrups and Baranova reached up to pull him down.

Modine said, "I'll tell you. I'll design something and if someone here can help me construct it according to the design, I'll try to fly. If I use my design and *I* can fly, then anyone can."

"I should think so, Mr. Modine," said Baranova, in a tone that seemed suspended between scepticism and hope.

—from "For the Birds"

THE ASIMOV CHRONICLES

CHRONICLES

FIFTY YEARS OF ISAAC ASIMOV!

V O L U M E   S I X

EDITED BY MARTIN H. GREENBERG

ACE BOOKS, NEW YORK

The stories in this collection are taken from an omnibus edition published in hardcover by Dark Harvest in 1989, titled *The Asimov Chronicles: Fifty Years of Isaac Asimov*.

THE ASIMOV CHRONICLES
VOLUME SIX

An Ace Book / published by arrangement with
Dark Harvest

PRINTING HISTORY
Dark Harvest edition published 1989
Ace edition / June 1991

ISBN: 0-441-03112-9

Ace Books are published by The Berkley Publishing Group,
200 Madison Avenue, New York, New York 10016.
The name ''ACE'' and the ''A'' logo
are trademarks belonging to Charter Communications, Inc.

PRINTED IN THE UNITED STATES OF AMERICA

10 9 8 7 6 5 4 3 2 1

CONTENTS

THE ASIMOV CHRONICLES

FIFTY YEARS OF ISAAC ASIMOV!

V O L U M E   S I X

FOUND!

Computer-Two, like the other three that chased each other's tails in orbit round the Earth, was much larger than it had to be.

It might have been one tenth its diameter and yet contained all the volume it needed to store the accumulated and accumulating data needed to control space flight.

They needed the extra space, however, so that Joe and I could get inside, if we had to.

And we had to.

Computer-Two was perfectly capable of taking care of itself. Ordinarily, that is. It was redundant. It worked everything out three times in parallel and all three programs had to mesh perfectly; all three answers had to match. If they did not, the answer was delayed for nano-seconds while Computer-Two checked itself, found the malfunctioning part and replaced it.

There was no sure way in which ordinary people would know how many times it caught itself. Perhaps never. Perhaps twice a day. Only Computer-Central could measure

1

the time delay induced by error and only Computer-Central knew how many of the component spares had been used as replacements. And Computer-Central never talked about it. The only good public image is perfection.

And for all practical purposes, it's *been* perfection, for there was never any call for Joe and me.

We're the trouble-shooters. We go up there when something really goes wrong and Computer-Two or one of the others can't correct itself. It's never happened in the five years we've been on the job. It did happen now and again in the early days of their existence, but that was before our time.

We keep in practice. Don't get me wrong. There isn't a computer made that Joe and I can't diagnose. Show us the error and we'll show you the malfunction. Or Joe will, anyway. I'm not the kind who sings one's own praises.

Anyway, this time, neither of us could make the diagnosis.

The first thing that happened was that Computer-Two lost internal pressure. That's not unprecedented and it's certainly not fatal. Computer-Two can work in a vacuum after all. An internal atmosphere was established in the old days when it was expected there would be a steady flow of repairmen fiddling with it. And it's been kept up out of tradition. Who told you scientists aren't chained by tradition? In their spare time from being scientists, they're human, too.

From the rate of pressure loss, it was deduced that a gravel-sized meteoroid had hit Computer-Two. Its exact radius, mass and energy was reported by Computer-Two itself, using that rate of pressure loss, and a few other things, as data.

The second thing that happened was that the break was not sealed and the atmosphere was not regenerated. After that came the errors and they called us in.

It made no sense. Joe let a look of pain cross his homely face and said, "There must be a dozen things out of whack."

Someone at Computer-Central said, "The hunk of gravel ricocheted, very likely."

Joe said, "With that energy of entry, it would have passed right through the other side. No ricochets. Besides, even with ricochets, I figure it would have had to take some very unlikely strikes."

"Well, then, what do we do?"

Joe looked uncomfortable. I think that it was at this point that he realized what was coming. He had made it sound peculiar enough to require the trouble-shooters on the spot— and Joe had never been up in space. If he had told me once that his chief reason for taking the job was that he knew it meant he would never have to go up in space, he had told it to me 2^x times, with x a pretty high number.

So I said it for him. I said, "We'll have to go up there."

Joe's only way out would have been to say he didn't think he could handle the job, and I watched his pride slowly come out ahead of his cowardice. Not by much, you understand—by a nose, let's say.

To those of you who haven't been on a spaceship in the last fifteen years—and I suppose Joe can't be the only one— let me emphasize that the initial acceleration is the only troublesome thing. You can't get away from that, of course.

After that it's nothing, unless you want to count possible boredom. You're just a spectator. The whole thing is automated and computerized. The old romantic days of space pilots are gone totally. I imagine they'll return briefly when our space settlements make the shift to the asteroid belt as they constantly threaten to do—but then only until additional Computers are placed in orbit to set up the necessary additional capacity.

Joe held his breath throughout the acceleration, or at least he seemed to. (I must admit that I wasn't very comfortable myself. It was only my third trip. I've taken a couple of vacations on Settlement-Rho with my husband, but I'm not exactly a seasoned hand.)

After that, he was relieved for a while, but only for a while. He got despondent.

"I hope this thing knows where it's going," he said, pettishly.

I extended my arms forward, palms up, and felt the rest of me sway backward a bit in the zero-gravity field. "You," I said, "are a computer specialist. Don't you *know* it knows?"

"Sure, but Computer-Two is off."

"We're not hooked into Computer-Two," I said. "There are three others. And even if only one were left functional, it could handle all the space flights undertaken on an average day."

"All four might go off. If Computer-Two is wrong, what's to stop the rest?"

"Then we'll run this thing manually."

"You'll do it, I suppose? You know how—I think not?"

"So they'll talk me in."

"For the love of Eniac," he groaned.

There was no problem, actually. We moved out to Computer-Two as smooth as vacuum and less than two days after takeoff, we were placed into a parking orbit not ten meters behind it.

What was not so smooth was that, about twenty hours out, we got the news from Earth that Computer-Three was losing internal pressure. Whatever had hit Computer-Two was going to get the rest, and when all four were out, space flight would grind to a halt. It could be reorganized on a manual basis, surely, but that would take months at a minimum, possibly years, and there would be serious economic dislocation on Earth. Worse yet, several thousand people now out in space would surely die.

It wouldn't bear thinking of and neither Joe nor I talked about it, but it didn't make Joe's disposition sweeter and, let's face it, it didn't make me any happier.

Earth hung over 200,000 kilometers below us, but Joe didn't seem to be bothered by that. He was concentrating on his tether and was checking the cartridge in his reaction-gun. He wanted to make sure he could get to Computer-Two and back again.

You'd be surprised—if you've never tried it—how you can get your space legs if you absolutely have to. I wouldn't say there was nothing to it and we did waste half the fuel we used, but we finally reached Computer-Two. We hardly made any bump at all when we struck Computer-Two. (You hear it, of course, even in vacuum, because the vibration travels through the metalloid fabric of your space suits—but there was hardly any bump, just a whisper.)

Of course, our contact and the addition of our momentum altered the orbit of Computer-Two slightly, but tiny expenditures of fuel compensated for that and we didn't have to worry about it. Computer-Two took care of it, for nothing had gone wrong with it, as far as we could tell, that affected any of its external workings.

We went over the outside first, naturally. The chances were pretty overwhelming that a small piece of gravel had whizzed through Computer-Two and that would leave an unmistakable ragged hole. Two of them in all probability; one going in and one coming out.

Chances of that happening are one in two million on any given day—even money that it will happen at least once in six thousand years. It's not likely, but it can, you know. The chances are one in not‧more than ten billion that, on any one day, it will be struck by a meteoroid large enough to demolish it.

I didn't mention that because Joe might realize that we were exposed to similar odds ourselves. In fact, any given strike on us would do far more damage to our soft and tender bodies than to the stoical and much-enduring machinery of the computer, and I didn't want Joe more nervous than he was.

The thing is, though, it wasn't a meteoroid.

"What's this?" said Joe, finally.

It was a small cylinder stuck to the outer wall of Computer-Two, the first abnormality we had found in its outward appearance. It was about half a centimeter in diameter and perhaps six centimeters long. Just about cigarette-sized for any of you who've been caught up in the antique fad of smoking.

We brought our small flashlights into play.

I said, "That's not one of the external components."

"It sure isn't," muttered Joe.

There was a faint spiral marking running round the cylinder from one end to the other. Nothing else. For the rest, it was clearly metal, but of an odd, grainy texture—at least to the eye.

Joe said, "It's not tight."

He touched it gently with a fat and gauntleted finger and it gave. Where it had made contact with the surface of Computer-Two, it lifted and our flashes shone down on a visible gap.

"There's the reason gas pressure inside declined to zero," I said.

Joe grunted. He pushed a little harder and the cylinder dropped away and began to drift. We managed to snare it after a little trouble. Left behind was a perfectly round hole in the skin of Computer-Two, half a centimeter across.

Joe said, "This thing, whatever it is, isn't much more than foil."

It gave easily under his fingers, thin but springy. A little extra pressure and it dented. He put it inside his pouch, which he snapped shut, and said, "Go over the outside and see if there are any other items like that anywhere on it. I'll go inside."

It didn't take me very long. Then I went in. "It's clean," I said. "That's the only thing there is. The only hole."

"One is enough," said Joe, gloomily. He looked at the smooth aluminum of the wall and, in the light of the flash, the perfect circle of black was beautifully evident.

• • •

It wasn't difficult to place a seal over the hole. It was a little more difficult to reconstitute the atmosphere. Computer-Two's reserve gas-forming supplies were low and the controls required manual adjustment. The solar generator was limping but we managed to get the lights on.

Eventually, we removed our gauntlets and helmet, but Joe carefully placed the gauntlets inside his helmet and secured them both to one of his suit-loops.

"I want these handy if the air pressure begins to drop," he said, sourly.

So I did the same. No use being devil-may-care.

There was a mark on the wall just next to the hole. I had noted it in the light of my flash when I was adjusting the seal. When the lights came on, it was obvious.

"You notice that, Joe?" I said.

"I notice."

There was a slight, narrow depression in the wall, not very noticeable at all, but it was there beyond doubt if you ran your finger over it and it continued for nearly a meter. It was as though someone had scooped out a very shallow sampling of the metal and the surface where that had taken place was distinctly less smooth than elsewhere.

I said, "We'd better call Computer-Central downstairs."

"If you mean back on Earth, say so," said Joe. "I hate that phony space-talk. In fact, I hate everything about space. That's why I took an Earth-side job—I mean a job on Earth—or what was supposed to be one."

I said patiently, "We'd better call Computer-Central back on Earth."

"What for?"

"To tell them we've found the trouble."

"Oh? What did we find?"

"The hole. Remember?"

"Oddly enough, I do. And what caused the hole? It wasn't a meteoroid. I never saw one that would leave a perfectly circular hole with no signs of buckling or melting. And I never saw one that left a cylinder behind." He took the cylinder out of his suit pocket and smoothed the dent out of its thin metal, thoughtfully. "Well, what caused the hole?"

I didn't hesitate. I said, "I don't know."

"If we report to Computer-Central, they'll ask the question and we'll say we don't know and what will we have gained? Except hassle?"

"They'll call us, Joe, if we don't call them."

"Sure. And we won't answer, will we?"

"They'll assume something killed us, Joe, and they'll send up a relief party."

"You know Computer-Central. It will take them at least two days to decide on that. We'll have something before then and once we have something, we'll call them."

The internal structure of Computer-Two was not *really* designed for human occupancy. What was foreseen and allowed for was the occasional and temporary presence of trouble-shooters. That meant there was room for maneuvering and there were tools and supplies.

There weren't any armchairs, though. For that matter, there was no gravitational field, either, or any centrifugal imitation of one.

We both floated in midair, drifting very slowly this way or that. Occasionally, one of us touched the wall and rebounded very slowly. Or else part of one of us overlapped part of the other.

"Keep your foot out of my mouth," said Joe, and pushed it away violently. It was a mistake because we both began to turn. Of course, that's not how it looked to us. To us, it was the interior of Computer-Two that was turning, which was most unpleasant, and it took us a while to get relatively motionless again.

We had the theory perfectly worked out in our Earth-side training, but we were short on practice. A lot short.

By the time we had steadied ourselves, I felt unpleasantly nauseated. You can call it nausea, or astronausea, or space sickness, but whatever you call it, it's the heaves and it's worse in space than anywhere else, because there's nothing to pull the stuff down. It floats around in a cloud of globules and you don't want to be floating around with it.—So I held it back, and so did Joe.

I said, "Joe, it's clearly the computer that's at fault. Let's get at its insides." Anything to get my mind off *my* insides and let them quiet down. Besides, things weren't moving fast enough. I kept thinking of Computer-Three on its way down the tube: maybe Computers-One and -Four by now, too; and thousands of people in space with their lives hanging on what we could do.

Joe looked a little greenish, too, but he said, "First I've got to think. Something got it. It wasn't a meteoroid, because whatever it was chewed a neat hole out of the hull. It wasn't cut out because I didn't find a circle of metal anywhere inside here. Did you?"

"No. But it hadn't occurred to me to look."

"I looked, and it's nowhere in here."

"It may have fallen outside."

"With the cylinder covering the hole till I pulled it away? A likely thing. Did you see anything come flying out?"

"No."

Joe said, "We may still find it in here, of course, but I doubt it. It was somehow dissolved and something got in."

"What something? Whose is it?"

Joe's grin was remarkably ill-natured. "Why do you bother asking questions to which there is no answer. If this was last century, I'd say the Russians had somehow stuck that device onto the outside of Computer-Two.—No offense. If it were last century, you'd say it was the Americans."

I decided to be offended. I said, coldly, "We're trying to say something that makes sense *this* century, Iosif," giving it an exaggerated Russian pronunciation.

"We'll have to assume some dissident group."

"If so," I said, "we'll have to assume one with a capacity

for space flight and with the ability to come up with an unusual device.''

Joe said, "Space flight presents no difficulties, if you can tap into the orbiting Computers illegally—which has been done. As for the cylinder, that may make more sense when it is analyzed back on Earth—downstairs, as you space buffs would say."

"It doesn't make sense," I said. "Where's the point in trying to disable Computer-Two?"

"As part of a program to cripple space flight."

"Then everyone suffers. The dissidents, too."

"But it gets everyone's attention, doesn't it, and suddenly the cause of whatever-it-is makes news. Or the plan is to just knock out Computer-Two and then threaten to knock out the other three. No real damage, but lots of potential, and lots of publicity."

"I don't believe it," I said. "It's too dramatic."

"On the contrary," said Joe. "I'm trying to be nondramatic." He was studying all parts of the interior closely, edging over it square centimeter by square centimeter. "I *might* suppose the thing was of nonhuman origin."

"Don't be silly."

"You want me to make the case? The cylinder made contact, after which something inside ate away a circle of metal and entered Computer-Two. It crawled over the inside wall eating away a thin layer of metal for some reason. Does that sound like anything of human construction?"

"Not that I know of, but I don't know everything. Even you don't know everything."

Joe ignored that. "So the question is, how did it—whatever it is—get into the computer, which is, after all, reasonably well-sealed. It did so quickly, since it knocked out the resealing and air-regeneration capacities almost at once."

"Is *that* what you're looking for?" I said, pointing.

He tried to stop too quickly and somersaulted backward, crying, "That's it! That's it!"

In his excitement, he was thrashing his arms and legs which got him nowhere, of course. I grabbed him and, for a while, we were both trying to exert pushes in uncoordinated directions and that got us nowhere either. Joe called me a few names, but I called him some back and I had the advantage of him there. I understand English perfectly, better than he does, in fact; but his knowledge of Russian is— well, fragmentary would be a kind of way of putting it. Bad language in an ununderstood language always sounds very dramatic.

"Here it is," he said, when we had finally sorted ourselves out.

Where the computer-shielding met the wall, there was a small circular hole left behind when Joe brushed aside a small cylinder. It was just like the one on the outer hull, but it seemed even thinner. In fact, it seemed to disintegrate when Joe touched it.

"We'd better get into the computer," said Joe.

The computer was a shambles.

Not obviously. I don't mean to say it was like a beam of wood that had been riddled by termites.

In fact, if you looked at the computer casually, you might swear it was intact.

Look closely, though, and some of the chips would be gone. The more closely you looked, the more you realized were gone. Worse yet, the stores which Computer-Two used in self-repair had dwindled to almost nothing. We kept looking and every once in a while, one of us would discover something else was missing.

Joe took the cylinder out of his pouch again and turned it end for end. He said, "I suspect it's after high-grade silicon in particular. I can't say for sure, of course, but my guess is that the sides are mostly aluminum but that the flat end is mostly silicon."

I said, "Do you mean the thing is a solar battery?"

"Part of it is. That's how it gets its energy in space;

energy to get to Computer-Two, energy to eat a hole into it, energy to—to—I don't know how else to put it. Energy to stay alive.''

''You call it alive?''

''Why not? Look, Computer-Two can repair itself. It can reject faulty bits of equipment and replace it with working ones, but it needs a supply of spares to work with. Given enough spares of all kinds, it could build a Computer just like itself, when properly programmed—but it needs the supply, so we don't think of it as alive. This object that entered Computer-Two is apparently collecting its own supplies. That's suspiciously life-like.''

''What you're saying,'' I said, ''is that we have here a microcomputer advanced enough to be considered alive.''

''I don't honestly know what I'm saying,'' said Joe.

''Who on Earth could make such a thing?''

''Who *on Earth*?''

I made the next discovery. It looked like a stubby pen drifting through the air. I just caught it out of the corner of my eye and it registered as a pen.

In zero gravity, things will drift out of pockets and float off. There's no way of keeping anything in place unless it is physically confined. You expect pens and coins and anything else that can find an opening to drift their way through the opening eventually and go wherever air currents and inertia lead them.

So my mind registered ''Pen'' and I groped for it absently and, of course, my fingers didn't close on it. Just reaching for something sets up an air current that pushes it away. You have to reach over it and sneak behind it with one hand, and then reach for it with the other. Picking up any small object in midair is a two-hand operation.

I know some people can do it one-handed, but they're space hounds and I'm not.

I turned to look at the object and pay a little more attention to retrieval, then realized that my pen was safely in its pouch. I felt for it and it was there.

"Did you lose a pen, Joe?" I called out.

"No."

"Anything like that? Key? Cigarette?"

"I don't smoke. You know that."

A stupid answer. "Anything?" I said in exasperation. "I'm seeing things here."

"No one ever said you were stable."

"Look, Joe. Over there. Over there."

He lunged for it. I could have told him it would do no good.

By now, though, our poking around in the computer seemed to have stirred things up. We were seeing them wherever we looked. They were floating in the air currents.

I stopped one at last. Or, rather, it stopped itself, for it was on the elbow of Joe's suit. I snatched it off and shouted. Joe jumped in terror and nearly knocked it out of my hand.

I said, "Look!"

There was a shiny circle on Joe's suit where I had taken the thing off. It had begun to eat its way through.

"Give it to me," said Joe. He took it gingerly and put it against the wall to hold it steady. Then he shelled it, gently lifting the paper-thin metal.

There was something inside that looked like a line of cigarette ash. It caught the light and glinted, though, like lightly woven metal.

There was a moistness about it, too. It wriggled slowly, one end seeming to seek something blindly.

The end made contact with the wall and stuck. Joe's finger pushed it away. It seemed to require a small effort to do so. Joe rubbed his finger and thumb and said, "Feels oily."

The metal worm—I don't know what else I can call it— seemed limp now after Joe had touched it. It didn't move again.

I was twisting and turning, trying to look at myself.

"Joe," I said, "for heaven's sake, have I got one of them on me anywhere?"

"I don't see one," he said.

"Well, *look* at me. You've got to watch me, Joe, and I'll watch you. If our suits are wrecked we might not be able to get back to the ship."

Joe said, "Keep moving, then."

It was a grisly feeling, being surrounded by things hungry to dissolve your suit wherever they could touch it. When any showed up, we tried to catch them and stay out of their way at the same time, which made things almost impossible. A rather long one drifted close to my leg and I kicked at it, which was stupid, for if I had hit it, it might have stuck. As it was, the air current I set up brought it against the wall, where it stayed.

Joe reached hastily for it—too hastily. The rest of his body rebounded and as he somersaulted, one booted foot struck the wall near the cylinder lightly. When he finally managed to right himself, it was still there.

"I didn't smash it, did I?"

"No, you didn't," I said. "You missed it by a decimeter. It won't get away."

I had a hand on either side of it. It was twice as long as the other cylinder had been. In fact, it was like two cylinders stuck together lengthwise, with a constriction at the point of joining.

"Act of reproducing," said Joe as he peeled away the metal. This time what was inside was a line of dust. Two lines. One on either side of the constriction.

"It doesn't take much to kill them," said Joe. He relaxed visibly. "I think we're safe."

"They do seem alive," I said, reluctantly.

"I think they seem more than that. They're viruses.— Or the equivalent."

"What are you talking about?"

Joe said, "Granted I'm a computer technologist and not a virologist—but it's my understanding that viruses on

Earth, or, downstairs, as you would say, consist of a nucleic acid molecule coated in a protein shell.

"When a virus invades a cell, it manages to dissolve a hole in the cell wall or membrane by the use of some appropriate enzyme and the nucleic acid slips inside, leaving the protein coat outside. Inside the cell it finds the material to make a new protein coat for itself. In fact, it manages to form replicas of itself and to form a new protein coat for each replica. Once it has stripped the cell of all it has, the cell dissolves and in place of the one invading virus there are several hundred daughter viruses. Sound familiar?"

"Yes. Very familiar. It's what's happening here. But where did it come from, Joe?"

"Not from Earth, obviously, or any Earth settlement. From somewhere else, I suppose. They drift through space till they find something appropriate in which they can multiply. They look for sizable objects ready-made of metal. I don't imagine they can smelt ores."

"But large metal objects with pure silicon components and a few other succulent matters like that are the products of intelligent life only," I said.

"Right," said Joe, "which means we have the best evidence yet that intelligent life is common in the Universe, since objects like the one we're on must be quite common or it couldn't support these viruses. And it means that intelligent life is old, too, perhaps ten billion years old—long enough for a kind of metal evolution, forming a metal/silicon/oil life as we have formed a nucleic/protein/water life. Time to evolve a parasite on space-age artifacts."

I said, "You make it sound as though every time some intelligent life form develops a space culture, it is subjected before long to parasitic infestation."

"Right. And it must be controlled. Fortunately, these things are easy to kill, especially now when they're forming. Later on, when they're ready to burrow out of Computer-Two, I suppose they will grow, thicken their shells, stabilize their interior and prepare, as the equivalent of spores, to drift a million years before they find another home. They might not be so easy to kill, then.''

''How are you going to kill them?''

''I already have. I just touched that first one when it instinctively sought out metal to begin manufacturing a new shell after I had broken open the first one—and that touch finished it. I didn't touch the second, but I kicked the wall near it and the sound vibration in the metal shook its interior apart into metal dust. So they can't get us, now, or any more of the computer if we just shake them apart now!''

He didn't have to explain further—or as much. He put on his gauntlets slowly, and then banged at the wall with one. It pushed him away and he kicked at the wall where he next approached it.

''You do the same,'' he shouted.

I tried to, and for a while we both kept at it. You don't know how hard it is to hit a wall at zero gravity, at least on purpose, and do it hard enough to make it clang. We missed as often as not or just struck it a glancing blow that sent us whirling but made virtually no sound. We were panting with effort and aggravation in no time.

But we had acclimated ourselves (or at least I had) and the nausea didn't return. We kept it up and then when we gathered up some more of the viruses, there was nothing inside but dust in every case. They were clearly adapted to empty, automated space objects which, like modern computers, were vibration-free. That's what made it possible, I suppose, to build up the exceedingly rickety complex metallic structures that possessed sufficient instability to produce the properties of simple life.

I said, ''Do you think we got them all, Joe?''

''How can I say? If there's one left, it will cannibalize the others for metal supplies and start all over. Let's bang around some more.''

We did until we were sufficiently worn out not to care whether one was still left alive.

"Of course," I said, panting, "the Planetary Association for the Advancement of Science isn't going to be pleased with our killing them all."

Joe's suggestion as to what the P.A.A.S. could do with itself was forceful, but impractical. He said, "Look, our mission is to save Computer-Two, a few thousand lives and, as it turned out, our own lives, too. Now they can decide whether to renovate this computer or rebuild it from scratch. It's their baby.

"The P.A.A.S. can get what they can out of these dead objects and that should be something. If they want live ones, I suspect they'll find them floating about in these regions. They can look for them if they want live specimens, but they'd better watch their suits at all times. I don't think they can vibrate them to death in open space."

I said, "All right. My suggestion is we tell Computer-Central we're going to jerry-rig this Computer and get it doing some work anyway, and we'll stay till a relief is up for main repairs or whatever in order to prevent any rein-festation. Meanwhile, they better get to each of the other Computers and set up a system that can set it to vibrating strongly as soon as the internal atmosphere shows a pressure drop."

"Simple enough," said Joe, sardonically.

"It's lucky we found them when we did."

"Wait awhile," said Joe, and the look in his eye was one of deep trouble. "We didn't find them. *They* found *us*. If metal life has developed, do you suppose it's likely that this is the only form it takes? Just this fragile kind?

"What if such life forms communicate somehow and, across the vastness of space, others are now converging on us for the picking? Other species, too; all of them after the lush new fodder of an as yet untouched space culture. *Other* species! Some that are sturdy enough to withstand vibration. Some that are large enough to be more versatile in their reactions to danger. Some that are equipped to invade our settlements in orbit. Some, for the sake of Univac, that may be able to invade the Earth for the metals of its cities.

"What I'm going to report, what I must report, is that we've been *found*!"

NOTHING FOR NOTHING

The scene was Earth.

Not that the beings on the starship thought of it as Earth. To them it was a series of symbols stored in a computer; it was the third planet of a star located at a certain position with respect to the line connecting their home planet with the black hole that marked the Galaxy's center, and moving at a certain velocity with reference to it.

The time was 15000 B.C., more or less.

Not that the beings on the starship thought of it as 15000 B.C. To them, it was a certain period of time marked off according to their local system of measurement.

The captain of the starship said, rather petulantly, "This is a waste of time. The planet is largely frozen. Let us leave."

But the ship's explorer quietly said, "No, Captain," and that was that.

As long as a starship was in space, or in hyperspace for that matter, the captain was supreme, but place that ship in

19

orbit about a planet and the explorer could not be challenged. He knew worlds! That was his specialty.

And this explorer was in an impregnable position. He had what amounted to a sure instinct for profitable trade. It had been he and he alone who was responsible for the fact that this particular starship had won three Awards for Excellence for the work done in its three last expeditions. Three for three.

So when the explorer said, "No," the captain could not dream of "Yes." Even in the unlikely case that he had, the crew would have mutinied. An Award for Excellence might be, to the captain, a pleasant spectral disk to suspend in the main salon, but to the crew it meant a spectacular addition to take-home pay and an even more welcome addition to vacation time and pension benefits. And this explorer had brought them that three times. Three for three.

The explorer said, "No strange world should be left unexamined."

The captain said, "What is strange about this one?"

"The preliminary probe shows intelligence, and on a frozen world."

"Surely that's not unprecedented."

"The pattern here is strange," the explorer looked uneasy. "I am not sure exactly how or exactly why, but the pattern of life and of intelligence is strange. We must examine it more carefully."

And that was that, of course. There were at least half a trillion planetary worlds in the Galaxy, if one only counted those associated with stars. Add to that the indefinite number moving independently through space and the number might be ten times as great.

Even with computers to help, no starship could know them all, but an experienced explorer, by dint of lacking interest in anything else, of studying every exploratory report published, of considering endless correlations, and, presumably, playing with statistics even in his sleep, grew to have what seemed to others a mystical intuition about such things.

"We'll have to send out probes in full interlocking program," said the explorer.

The captain looked outraged. Full power meant a leisurely examination for weeks at enormous expense.

He said, and it was as much as he could offer in the way of objection, "Is that absolutely necessary?"

"I rather think so," said the explorer with the self-confidence of one who knows his whim is law.

The probes brought back exactly what the captain expected, and in great detail. An intelligent species rather reminiscent, at least as far as superficial appearance went, of the lesser breeds of the inner proximal regions of the fifth arm of the Galaxy—not quite unusual, but of interest to mentologists, no doubt.

As yet the intelligent species was only at the first level of technology—long, long removed from anything useful.

The captain said so, scarcely able to mask his exasperation, but the explorer, leafing through the reports, remained unmoved. He said, "Strange!" and asked that the trader be summoned.

This was really too much. A successful captain must never give a good explorer cause for unhappiness but there are limits to everything.

The captain said, fighting to keep the level of communication polite, if not friendly, "To what end, Explorer? What can we expect at this level?"

"They have tools," said the explorer thoughtfully.

"Stone! Bone! Wood! Or this planet's equivalent of that. And that's all. Surely we can find nothing in that."

"And yet there is something strange in the pattern."

"May I know what that might be, Explorer?"

"If I knew what it might be, Captain, it would not be strange, and I would not have to find out. Really, Captain, I must insist on the Trader."

• • •

The trader was as indignant as the captain was, and had more scope to express it. His, after all, was a speciality as deep as that of anyone's on the starship, even, in his own opinion (and in some other's), as deep and as essential as the explorer's.

The captain might navigate a starship and the explorer might detect useful civilizations by the most tenuous of signs, but in the final clutch it was the trader and his team who faced the aliens and who plucked out of their minds and culture that which was useful and gave in return something *they* found useful.

And this was done at great risk. The alien ecology must not be disrupted. Alien intelligences must not be harmed, not even to save one's own life. There were good reasons for that on the cosmic scale and traders were amply rewarded for the risks they ran, but why run *useless* risks.

The trader said, "There is nothing there. *My* interpretation of the probe's data is that we're dealing with semi-intelligent animals. Their usefulness is nil. Their danger is great. We know how to deal with truly intelligent aliens and trader teams are rarely killed by them. Who knows how these animals will react—and you know we are not allowed to defend ourselves properly."

The explorer said, "These animals, if they are no more than that, have interestingly adapted themselves to the ice. There are subtle variations in the pattern here I do not understand, but my considered opinion is that they will not be dangerous and that they may even be useful. I feel they are worth closer examination."

"What can be gained from a Stone Age intelligence?" asked the trader.

"That is for you to find out."

The trader thought grimly: Of course, that is what it comes to—for *us* to find out.

He knew well the history and purpose of the starship expeditions. There had been a time, a million years before, when there had been no traders, explorers, or captains but only ancestral animals with developing mind and a Stone Age technology—much like the animals on the world they were now orbiting. How slow the advance, how painfully slow the self-generated progress—until the third-level civilization had been reached. Then had come the starships and the chance of cross-fertilization of cultures. *Then* had come progress.

The trader said, "With respect, Explorer, I grant your intuitional experience. Will you grant my practical experience, though it is less dramatic? There is no way in which anything below a third-level civilization can have anything we can use."

"That," said the explorer, "is a generalization that may or may not be true."

"With respect, Explorer. It *is* true. And even if those—those semianimals had something we could use, and I can't imagine what it might be, what can we give them in exchange?"

The explorer was silent.

The trader went on. "At this level, there is no way in which a protointelligence can accept an alien stimulation. The mentologists are agreed on that and it is my experience, too. Progress *must* be self-generated until at least the second level is reached. And we *must* make a return; we can take nothing for nothing."

The captain said, "And that makes sense, of course. By stimulating these intelligences to advance, we can harvest them again at a later visit."

"I don't care about the reason for it," said the trader, impatiently. "It is part of the tradition of my profession. We do no harm under any conditions and we give a return for what we take. Here there is nothing we will want to take; and even if we find something, there will be nothing that we can give in return.—We waste time."

The explorer shook his head. "I ask you to visit some

center of population, Trader. I will abide by your decision when you return."

And that was that, too.

For two days the small trader module flashed over the surface of the planet searching for any evidence of a reasonable level of technology. There was none.

A complete search could take years but was scarcely worth it. It was unreasonable to suppose a high level would be hidden. The highest technology was always flaunted for it had no enemy. That was the universal experience of traders everywhere.

It was a beautiful planet, half-frozen as it was. White and blue and green. Wild and rough and variegated. Crude—and untouched.

But it was not the trader's job to deal with beauty and he shrugged off such thoughts impatiently. When his crew talked to him in such terms, he was short with them.

He said, "We'll land here. It seems to be a good-sized concentration of the intelligences. We can do no better."

His second said, "What can we do even with these, Maestro?"

"You can record," said the trader. "Record the animals, both unintelligent and supposedly intelligent, and any artifacts of theirs we can find. Make sure the records are thoroughly holographic."

"We can already see—" began the second.

"*We* can already see," said the trader, "but we must have a record to convince our explorer out of his dreams or we'll remain here forever."

"He is a good explorer," said one of the crew.

"He has been a good explorer," said the trader, "but does that mean he will be good forever? Perhaps his very successes have made him accept himself at too high an evaluation. So we must convince him of reality—if we can."

They wore their suits when they emerged from the module.

The planetary atmosphere would support them, but the feeling of exposure to the raw winds of an open planet would discommode them, even if the atmosphere and temperature were perfect—which they weren't. The gravity was a touch high, as was the light level, but they could bear it.

The intelligent beings, dressed rather sketchily in the outer portions of other animals, retreated reluctantly at their approach and watched at a distance. The trader was relieved at this. Any sign of nonbelligerence was welcome to those not permitted to defend themselves.

The trader and his crew did not try to communicate directly or to make friendly gestures. Who knew what gesture might be considered friendly by an alien? The trader set up a mental field, instead, and saturated it with the vibrations of the harmlessness and peace and hoped that the mental fields of the creatures were sufficiently advanced to respond.

Perhaps they were, for a few crept back and watched motionlessly as though intensely curious. The trader thought he detected fugitive thoughts—but that seemed unlikely for first-level beings and he did not follow them up.

Instead, he went stolidly about the business of making holographic reproductions of the vegetation, of a herd of blundering herbivores that appeared and then, deciding the surroundings were dangerous, thundered away. A large animal stood its ground for a while, exposing white weapons in a cavity at its force-end—then left.

The trader's crew worked as he did, moving methodically across the landscape.

The call, directly mental, and surcharged with such emotion of surprise and awe that the informational content was all but blurred out, came unexpectedly.

"Maestro! Here! Come quickly!"

Specific directions were not given. The trader had to

follow the beam, which led into a crevice bounded by two rocky outcroppings.

Other members of the crew were converging but the trader had arrived first.

"What is it?" asked the trader.

His second was standing in the glow of his suit-radiation in a deeply hollowed-out portion of the hillside.

The trader looked about. "This is a natural hollow, not a technological product."

"Yes, but look!"

The trader looked up and for perhaps five seconds he was lost. Then he sent out a strenuous message for all others to stay away.

He said, "Is this of technological origin?"

"Yes, Maestro. You can see it is only partly completed."

"But by whom?"

"By those creatures out there. The intelligent ones. I found one at work in here. This is his light source; it was burning vegetation. These are his tools."

"And where is he?"

"He fled."

"Did you actually see him?"

"I recorded him."

The trader pondered. Then he looked up again. "Have you ever seen anything like this?"

"No, Maestro."

"Or heard of anything like this?"

"No, Maestro."

"Astonishing!"

The trader showed no signs of wanting to withdraw his eyes, and the second said, softly, "Maestro, what do we do?"

"Eh?"

"This will surely win our ship still a fourth prize."

"Surely," said the trader, regretfully, "if we could take it."

The second said, hesitantly, "I have already recorded it."

"Eh? What is the use of that? We have nothing to give in exchange."

"But we have this. Give them anything."

The trader said, "What are you saying? They are too primitive to accept anything we could give them. It will surely be nearly a million years before they could possibly accept the suggestions of exogenous origin.—We will have to destroy the recording."

"But we *know*, Maestro."

"Then we must never talk about it. Our craft has its ethics and its traditions. You know that. Nothing for nothing!"

"Even this?"

"Even this."

The trader's sternly implacable set of expression was tinged with unbearable sorrow and despite his "Even this" he stood irresolute.

The second sensed that. He said, "*Try* giving them something, Maestro."

"Of what use would that be?"

"Of what harm?"

The trader said, "I have prepared a presentation for the entire starship, but I must show it to you first, Explorer—with deep respect and with apologies for masked thoughts. You were right. There *was* something strange about this planet. Though the intelligences on the planet were barely first level and though their technology was primitive in the extreme, they had developed a concept we have never had and one that, to my knowledge, we have never encountered on any other world."

The captain said, uneasily, "I cannot imagine what it might be." He was quite aware that traders sometimes overpraised their purchases to magnify their own worth.

The explorer said nothing. He was the more uneasy of the two.

The trader said, "It is a form of visual art."

"Playing with color?" asked the captain.

"And shape—but to most startling effect." He had arranged the holographic projector. "Observe!"

In the viewing space before them, a herd of animals appeared; bulky, shaggy, two-horned, four-legged. They hesitated, then ran, dust spurting up beneath their hooves.

"Ugly objects," muttered the captain.

The holographic recording brought the herd to a halt, clamped it down to a still. It magnified, and a single beast filled the view, its bulky head lowered, its nostrils distended.

"Observe this animal," said the trader, "and now observe this artificial composition of a primitive concoction of oil and colored mineral, which we found smeared over the roof of a cave."

There it was again! Not quite the animal as holographed— flat, but vibrant.

"What a peculiar similarity," said the captain.

"Not peculiar," said the trader. "Deliberate! There were dozens of such figures in different poses—of different animals. The likenesses were too detailed to be fortuitous. Imagine the boldness of the conception—to place colors in pleasing shapes and combinations, and in such a way as to deceive the eye into thinking it is looking at a real object. These organisms have devised an art that represents reality. It is representational art, as I suppose we might call it.

"And that's not all. We found it done in three dimensions also." The trader produced an array of small figures in gray stone and in faintly yellow bone. "These are clearly intended to represent themselves."

The captain seemed stupefied. "Did you see these manufactured?"

"No, that I did not, Captain. One of my men saw a planetary being smearing color on one of the cave representations, but these we found already formed. Still, no other explanation is possible than that they were deliberately shaped. These objects could not have assumed these shapes by chance processes.''

The captain said, ''These are curious, but one doesn't follow the motive. Would not holographic techniques serve the purpose better—at such times as these are developed, of course?''

''These primitives have no conception that holography could someday be developed and could not wait the million years required. Then, too, maybe holography is *not* better. If you compare the representations with the originals you will notice that the representations are simplified and distorted in subtle ways designed to bring certain characteristics into focus. I believe this form of art *improves* on the original in some ways and certainly has something different to say.''

The trader turned to the explorer. ''I stand in awe at your abilities. Can you explain how you sensed the uniqueness of this intelligence?''

The explorer signed a negative. ''I did not suspect this at all. It is interesting and I see its worth—although I wonder if we could ourselves properly control our colors and shapes in order to force them into such representational form. Yet this does match the unease within me.—What I wonder is how you came into possession of these? What did you give in exchange? It is *there* I see the strangeness lie.''

''Well,'' said the trader, ''in a way you're right. Quite strange. I did not think I could give anything since the organisms are so primitive, but this discovery seemed too important to sacrifice without some effort. I therefore chose from among the group of beings who formed these objects one whose mental field seemed somewhat more intense than that of the others and attempted to transfer to him a gift in exchange.''

''And succeeded. Of course,'' said the explorer.

''Yes, I succeeded,'' said the trader, happily, failing to notice that the explorer had made a statement and had not asked a question. ''The beings,'' the trader went on, ''kill such animals as they represent in color, by throwing long sticks tipped with sharpened stone. These penetrate the hide of the animals, wound and weaken them. They can then be killed by the beings who are individually smaller and weaker than the animal they hunt. I pointed out that a smaller, stone-tipped stick could be hurled forward with greater force and effect and with longer range if a cord under tension were used as the mechanism of propulsion.''

The explorer said, ''Such devices have been encountered among primitive intelligences which were, however, far advanced beyond these. Paleomentologists call it a bow and arrow.''

The captain said, ''How could the knowledge be absorbed? It couldn't be, at this level of the development.''

''But it *was*. Unmistakably. The response of the mental field was one of insight at almost unbearable intensity.— Surely you do not think I would have taken these art objects, were they twenty times as valuable, if I had not been convinced that I had made a return? Nothing for nothing, Captain.''

The explorer said in a low, despondent voice, ''There is the strangeness. To accept.''

The captain said, ''But surely, Trader, we cannot do this. They are not ready. We are harming them. They will use the bow and arrow to wound each other and not the beasts alone.''

The trader said, ''*We* do not harm them and we *did* not harm them. What *they* do to each other and where they end as a result, a million years from now, is not our concern.''

The captain and the trader left to set up the demonstration for the starship's company, and the explorer said sadly in the direction in which they had gone, ''But they accepted. And they flourish amid the ice. And in twenty thousand years, it will be *our* concern.''

He knew they would not believe him, and he despaired.

FOR THE BIRDS

Charles Modine, despite the fact that he was in his late thirties, and in perfect health, had never been in space. He had seen space settlements on television and had occasionally read about them in the public prints but it went no further than that.

To tell the truth, he was not interested in space. He had been born on Earth, and Earth was enough for him. When he wanted a change of environment, he turned to the sea. He was an avid and skilled sailor.

He was therefore repelled when the representative of Space Structures, Limited, finally told him that in order for him to do the job they were asking him to do, he would have to leave Earth.

Modine said, "Listen. I'm not a space person. I design clothes. What do I know about rockets and acceleration and trajectories and all the rest of it?"

"*We* know about that. You don't have to," said the other, urgently. Her name was Naomi Baranova and she had the queer, tentative walk of someone who had been in space so long she wasn't sure what the gravitational situation was at the moment.

Her clothes, Modine noted with some irritation, functioned as coverings and as little else. A tarpaulin would have done as well.

"But why need I come out to a space station?" he said.

"For what *you* know. We want you to design something for us."

"Clothes?"

"Wings."

Modine thought about it. He had a high, pale forehead and the process of thought always seemed to flush it somewhat. He had been told that at any rate. This time, if it flushed, it was partly in annoyance. "I can do that here, can't I?"

Baranova shook her head firmly. She had hair with a dark reddish tinge that was slowly being invaded by gray. She didn't seem to mind. She said, "We want you to understand the situation, Mr. Modine. We've consulted the technicians and the computer experts and they've built the most efficient possible wings, they tell us. They've taken into account stresses and surfaces and flexibilities and maneuverabilities and everything else you can imagine—but it doesn't help. We think perhaps a few frills—"

"Frills, Ms. Baranova?"

"Something other than scientific perfection. Something to rouse interest. Otherwise, the space settlements won't survive. That's why I want you there; to appreciate the situation for yourself. We're prepared to pay you very well."

It was the promised pay, including a healthy retainer, win or lose, that brought Modine into space. He was no more money-mad than the average human being, but he was not money-insensitive either, and he liked to see his reputation appreciated.

Nor was it actually as bad as he had expected. In the

early days of space travel, there had been short periods of high acceleration and long cramped periods in small modules. Somehow that was what Earth-bound people still thought of in connection with space travel. But a century had passed and the shuttles were commodious, while the hydraulic seats seemed to sop up the acceleration as though it were nothing more than a coffee spill.

Modine spent the time studying photographs of the wings in action and in watching holographic videotapes of the flyers.

He said, "There's a certain grace to the performance."

Naomi Baranova smiled rather sadly. "You're watching experts—athletes. If you could see me trying to handle those wings and manage to tumble and sideslip, I'm afraid you would laugh. And yet I'm better than most."

They were approaching Space Settlement Five. Its name was Chrysalis, officially, but everyone called it Five.

"You might suppose," said Baranova, "that it would be the other way around, but there's no feeling of poetry about the place. That's the trouble. It's not a home; it's just a job, and it is hard to make people establish families and settle down. Until it's a home—"

Five showed up as a small sphere, far away, looking much as Modine had seen it on television on Earth. He knew it was larger than it looked, but that was only an intellectual knowledge. His eyes and his emotions were not prepared for the steady increase in size as they approached. The spaceship and he dwarfed steadily and, eventually, they were circling an enormous object of glass and aluminum.

He watched for a long time before he became aware that they were still circling. He said, "Aren't we going to land on it?"

"Not that easy," said Baranova. "Five rotates on an axis about once in two minutes. It has to in order to set up a centrifugal effect that will keep everything inside pressed against the inner wall and create an artificial gravity. We have to match that speed before we can land. It takes time.''

"Must it spin that quickly?''

"To have the centrifugal effect mimic Earth-strength gravity, yes. That's the basic problem. It would be much better if we could use a slow spin to produce a tenth-normal gravity or even less, but that interferes with human physiology. People can't take low gravity for too long.''

The ship's speed had nearly matched the rotation period of Five. Modine could clearly see the curve of the outer mirror that caught the sunlight and with it illuminated Five's interior. He could make out the solar power station that supplied the energy for the station, with enough left over for export to Earth.

And they finally entered at one of the poles of the sphere and were inside Five.

Modine had spent a full day on Five and he was tired—but he had, rather unexpectedly, enjoyed it. They were sitting now on lawn furniture—on a wide stretch of grass—against a vista of suburbia.

There were clouds overhead—sunshine, without a clear view of the Sun itself—a wind—and, in the distance, a small stream.

It was hard to believe he was on a sphere floating in space in the Moon's orbit, circling Earth once a month. He said, "It's like a world.''

Baranova said, "So it seems when you're new here. When you've been here a time, you discover you know every corner of it. Everything repeats.''

Modine said, "If you live in a particular town on Earth, everything repeats too.''

"I know. But on Earth you can travel widely if you wish. Even if you don't travel, you know you can. Here you can't. That's—not so good; but it's not the worst.''

"You don't have the Earth's worst," said Modine. "I'm sure you don't have weather extremes."

"The weather, Mr. Modine, is indeed Garden of Edenish, but you get used to that.—Let me show you something. I have a ball here. Could you throw it high up; straight up, and catch it?"

Modine smiled. "Are you serious?"

"Quite. Please do."

Modine said, "I'm not a ball player, but I think I can throw a ball. I might even catch it when it comes down."

He threw the ball upward. It curved parabolically, and Modine found himself drifting forward in order to catch it, then running. It fell out of reach.

Baranova said, "You didn't throw it straight up, Mr. Modine."

"Yes I did," gasped Modine.

"Only by Earth standards," said Baranova. "The difficulty is that what we call the Coriolis force is involved. Here at the inner surface of Five, we're moving quite rapidly in a great circle about the axis. If you throw the ball upward it moves nearer the axis where things make a smaller circle and move more slowly. However, the ball retains the speed it had down here, so it moves ahead and you couldn't catch it. If you had wanted to catch it, you would have had to throw it up and back so that it would loop and return to you like a boomerang. The details of motion are different here on Five than on Earth."

Modine said, thoughtfully, "You get used to it, I suppose."

"Not entirely. We live in the equatorial regions of our small sphere. That's where the motion is fastest and where we get the effect of normal gravity. If we move upward toward the axis, or along the surface toward the poles, the gravitational effect decreases rapidly. We frequently have to go up or poleward and, whenever we do, the Coriolis effect must be taken into account. We have small monorails that must move spirally toward either pole; one track pole-

ward, another returning. In the trip we feel ourselves per-
petually canted to one side. It takes a long time to get used
to it and some people never learn the trick of it. No one
likes to live here for that reason.''

"Can you do something about that twisting effect?''

"If we could make our rotation slower, we would lessen
the Coriolis, but we would also lessen the feel of gravitation
and we can't do that.''

"Damned if you do, damned if you don't.''

"Not entirely. We could get along with less gravitation,
if we exercise, but it would mean exercise every day for
considerable periods. That would have to be fun. People
won't indulge in daily calisthenics that are troublesome or
a bore. We used to think that flying would be the answer.
When we go to the low-gravity regions near the poles,
people are almost weightless. They can almost rise into the
air by flapping their arms. If we attach light plastic wings
to each arm, stiffened by flexible rods, and if those wings
are folded and extended in just the right rhythm, people can
fly like birds.''

"Will that work as exercise?''

"Oh, yes. Flying is hard work, I assure you. The arm
and shoulder muscles may not have to do much to keep
you aloft but they must be in continuous use to maneuver
you properly. It keeps up the muscle tone and bone cal-
cium, *if* it's done on a regular basis.—But people won't
do it.''

"I should think they'd love to fly.''

Baranova sniffed. "They would, if it were easy enough.
The trouble is that it requires skillful coordination of muscles
to keep steady. The slightest errors result in tumbling and
spinning and almost inevitable nausea. Some can learn how
to fly gracefully as you saw on the holo-cassettes, but very
few.''

"Birds don't get seasick.''

"Birds fly in normal gravity fields. People on Five don't."

Modine frowned and grew thoughtful.

Baranova said, "I can't promise that you'll sleep. People don't usually their first few nights on a space settlement. Still, please try to do so and tomorrow we'll go to the flying areas."

Modine could see what Baranova had meant by saying the Coriolis force was unpleasant. The small monorail coach that took them poleward seemed constantly to be sliding leftward and his entrails seemed to be doing the same. He held on to the handgrips, white-knuckled.

"I'm sorry," said Baranova, sympathetically. "If we went more slowly, it wouldn't be so bad, but we're holding up traffic as it is."

"Do you get used to this?" groaned Modine.

"Somewhat. Not enough."

He was glad to stop finally, but only limitedly so. It took a while to get used to the fact that he seemed to be floating. Each time he tried to move, he tumbled, and each time he tumbled he didn't fall but drifted slowly forward or upward and returned only gradually. His automatic kicking made things worse.

Baranova left him to himself for a while, then caught at him and drew him slowly back. "Some people enjoy this," she said.

"I don't," gasped Modine, miserably.

"Many don't. Please put your feet into these stirrups on the ground and don't make any sudden movements."

There were five of them flying in the sky. Baranova said, "Those five birds are here just about every day. There are a few hundred who are there now and then. We could accommodate at this pole and at the other, as well as along the axis, something like five thousand at a time. We could use all the space to keep Five's thirty thousand people in condition. What do we do?''

Modine gestured and his body swayed backward in response. "They must have learned how, those birds up there. They weren't born birds. Can't the others learn it, too?''

"Those up there have natural coordination.''

"What can I do then? I'm a fashion designer. I don't create natural coordination.''

"Not having natural coordination doesn't stop you altogether. It just means working hard, practicing longer. Is there any way you could make the process more—fashionable? Could you design a flying costume; suggest a psychological campaign to get the people out? If we could arrange proper programs of exercise and physical fitness, we could slow Five's rotation, weaken the Coriolis effect, make this place a home.''

"You may be asking for a miracle.—Could you have them come closer?''

Baranova waved and one of the birds saw her, and swooped toward them in a long graceful curve. It was a young woman. She hovered ten feet away, smiling, her wings flicking slightly at the tips.

"Hi," she called out. "What's up?''

"Nothing," said Baranova. "My friend wants to watch you handle the wings. Show him how they work.''

The young woman smiled and, twisting first one wing, then the other, performed a slow somersault. She straightened to a halt with both wings given a backhanded twist, then rose slowly, her feet dangling and her wings moving slowly. The wing motion grew more rapid and she was off in wild acceleration.

Modine said, after a while, "Rather like ballet dancing, but the wings are ugly.''

"Are they? Are they?''

"Certainly," said Modine. "They look like bat wings. The associations are all wrong."

"Tell us what to do then? Should we put a feather design on them? Would that bring out the fliers and make them try harder to learn?"

"No." Modine thought for a while. "Maybe we can make the whole process easier."

He took his feet out of the stirrups, gave himself a little push and floated into the air. He moved his arms and legs experimentally and rocked erratically. He tried to scramble back for the stirrups and Baranova reached up to pull him down.

Modine said, "I'll tell you. I'll design something and if someone here can help me construct it according to the design, I'll try to fly. I've never done any such thing; you've just seen me try to wriggle in the air and I can't even do that. Well, if I use my design and I can fly, then anyone can."

"I should think so, Mr. Modine," said Baranova, in a tone that seemed suspended between skepticism and hope.

By the end of the week, Modine was beginning to feel that Space Settlement Five was home. As long as he stayed at ground level in the equatorial regions, where the gravitational effect was normal, there was no Coriolis effect to bother him and he felt his surroundings to be very Earth-like.

"The first time out," he said, "I don't want to be watched by the population generally because it may be harder than I think and I don't want to get this thing off to a bad start.— But I would like to be watched by some of the officials of the Settlement, just in case I make it."

Baranova said, "I should think we would try in private first. A failure the first time, whatever the excuse—"

"But a success would be so impressive."

"What are the chances of success? Be reasonable."

"The chances are good, Ms. Baranova. Believe me. What

you have been doing here is all wrong. You're flying in air—like birds—and it's so hard. You said it yourself. Birds on Earth operate under gravity. The birds up here operate without gravity—so everything has to be designed differently.''

The temperature, as always, was perfectly adjusted. So was the humidity. So was the wind speed. The atmosphere was so perfect it was as though it weren't there.—And yet Modine was perspiring with a bad case of stage fright. He was also gasping. The air was thinner in these gravity-free regions than at the equator—not by much, but enough thinner for him to have trouble gathering enough with his heart pounding so.

The air was empty of the human birds; the audience was a handful—the Coordinator, the Secretary of Health, the Commissioner of Safety and so on. There were a dozen men and women present. Only Baranova was familiar.

He had been outfitted with a small mike and he tried to keep his voice from shaking.

He said, ''We are flying without gravity and neither birds nor bats are a good model for us. They fly *with* gravity.— It's different in the sea. There's little effective gravity in water, since buoyancy lifts you. When we fly through no-gravity water, we call it swimming. In Space Station Five, where there's no gravity in this region, the air is for swimming, not for flying. We must imitate the dolphin and not the eagle.''

He sprang into the air as he spoke, wearing a graceful one-piece suit that neither clung skintight nor bellied. He began to tumble at once, but stretching one arm was sufficient to activate a small gas cartridge. A smoothly curved fin emerged along his spinal column, while a shallow keel marked the line of his abdomen.

The tumbling ceased. ''Without gravity,'' he said, ''this is enough to stabilize your flight. You can still tip and turn, but always under control. I may not do it well at first, but it won't take much practice.''

He stretched his other arm and each foot was suddenly outlined by a flipper—each elbow by another.

''These,'' he said, ''offer the propulsive force. You needn't flap the arms. Gentle motions will suffice for everything, but you have to bend your body and arch your neck in order to make turns and veers. You have to twist and alter the angle of your arms and legs. The whole body is engaged, but smoothly and nonviolently.—Which is all the better, for every muscle in your body is involved and you can keep it up for hours without tiring.''

He could feel himself moving more surely and gracefully—and faster. Up, up, he was suddenly going, with the air rushing past him until he was almost in a panic for fear he would not be able to slow up. But he turned his heels and elbows almost instinctively and felt himself curve and slow.

Dimly, through the pounding of his heart, he could hear the applause.

Baranova said, admiringly, ''How did you see this when our technicians couldn't?''

''The technicians started with the inevitable assumption of wings, thanks to birds and airplanes, and designed the most efficient ones possible. That's a technician's job. The job of a fashion designer is to see things as an artistic whole. I could see that the wings didn't fit the conditions of the space settlement. Just my job.''

Baranova said, ''We'll make these dolphin suits and get the population out into the air. I'm sure we can now. And then we can lay our plans to begin to slow Five's rotation.''

''Or stop it altogether,'' said Modine. ''I suspect that everyone will want to swim all the time instead of walking.''

He laughed. "They may not ever want to walk again. I may not."

They made out the large check they had promised and Modine, smiling at the figure, said, "Wings are for the birds."

IGNITION POINT!

"Let me get this straight," said Anthony Myers, leaning across his desk toward the man in the chair facing him. "Your computer does *not* write the speech?"

"No, you do. Or someone else does." Nicholas Jansen was quite composed. He was a small man, very neatly dressed, with an old-fashioned knotted tie that did not seem to make him the least bit self-conscious in a world of turtlenecks.

He said, "What I have developed is a series of words, phrases, sentences that induce reactions in specific groups of people, divided by sex, age, ethnic groups, language, occupation, place of residence or almost anything else conceivable. If you could describe the audience your man would be addressing in sufficient detail, then I could supply you with precisely the sort of thing his talk should include. The more we know about the audience the more accurately my computer program can produce the key words and phrases. They are woven into a speech—"

"Can they? Will they make sense?"

43

"That's up to the ingenuity of the speech writer, but it doesn't really matter. If you're pounding a drum, you might get the audience stirred up until their feet and hearts are pounding with it; till they reach ignition point. Sense is analogous to tune, but a drum doesn't have to beat out a tune; it merely establishes a rhythm. You can put in as much tune as you can, but it is the rhythm you're after. Do you understand?"

Myers rubbed his chin and stared at the other thoughtfully. "Have you tried this before?"

Jansen smiled narrowly. "Only unofficially. In a small way. Still, I know what I'm talking about. I'm an ochologist—"

"A what?"

"A student of mob psychology, and the first, as far as I know, who has truly computerized the matter."

"And you know this will work—in theory."

"No, I know it *might* work—in theory."

"And you want to try it out on me. What if it doesn't work?"

"Then what have you to lose? I'm not charging you. It's useful in my work, and if I may believe what I have been told, your man is lost if you don't use my services."

Myers drummed his fingers on the desk softly. "Look. Let me explain about my man. He looks impressive. He's got a good voice. He's amiable and likable. Properly handled I can make him a corporation executive, or an ambassador, or the President of the United States. The trouble is he has no brains to speak of and he needs me to supply them. But the one thing he has to be able to do without me is to deliver a speech in such a way as to fool people into thinking he does have brains. This he cannot do, even if the speech is written out for him. The speech may be intelligent and yet he can't say it in such a way as to make *himself* seem intelligent. Do you think you can write a speech better than I can?"

"Not better. Just foolproof. I can make it possible for

him to push the right buttons and ignite the audience.''

"What do you mean, ignite?"

"To catch fire. Isn't that what ignite means? Every crowd has its ignition point, though every different crowd requires something different for ignition."

"You may be selling me a load of nonsense, Mr. Jansen. There's no speech so fool-proof that a nincompoop won't spoil it."

"On the contrary. A nincompoop might deliver it more surely than you could, since he won't be thinking for himself. May I meet him?—That is, if you want my services?"

"You understand that everything said here is confidential."

"Certainly. Since I intend to turn this to commercial use eventually, I am more interested in confidentiality than you are."

Barry Winston Bloch was not quite forty. He had played semipro baseball in his younger days. He had made his way through a midwestern college with minimal effort and he had been moderately successful as a salesman. His appearance was impressive, not because he was handsome but because he looked physically powerful, and gave the impression of possessing a mature wisdom. His hair was already showing streaks of gray and he had a way of throwing his head up and smiling warmly that filled you full of confidence in him.

It took an hour or so, usually, to realize that there was nothing behind the amiability but additional amiability.

Right now, Bloch felt uncomfortable. Ever since he had tied up with Myers, he had been a prey to discomfort. He wanted to get ahead; it was his secret desire to be a congressman and sometimes he wondered if he might not be a great evangelist, but the trouble was that people made him nervous. After he had used up his big grin, it came time to talk and he never had anything particular to say.

And no one had ever made him feel quite as uncomfortable as this little man with his gimlet eyes, who would sit there absolutely motionless while Bloch read his speeches. It was hard enough to talk to a real audience which rustled and coughed and seemed to be annoyed with him for not finishing. This little man—he had to remember his name was Jansen—who never responded in any way just choked him off.

No, he responded in one way—he invariably handed Bloch another speech to read. Each one was a little different and each one appealed to him somehow, but he never felt as if he did them justice. It made him sad somehow—and ashamed.

The manuscript presented to him on *this* day seemed worse than all the others. He looked at it in dismay. "What are all these marks?"

"Well now, B.B.," Myers adopted the soothing tone he almost always used with Bloch, "just let Mr. Jansen explain."

"It's direction. It's something you must learn, but it won't be difficult. A dash means a pause, an underlining means an emphasis. A downward arrow before a word means you let your voice drop a couple of notes; an upward arrow means you let it rise. A curved arrow means you let things fade off in contempt, if it curves downward. If it curves upward, your voice rises in anger. A parenthesis means a small smile; a double parenthesis means a grin; a triple parenthesis means a chuckle. You never laugh out loud. A line over a word means you look grim; a double line means you repeat. An asterisk—"

Bloch said, "I can't remember all that."

Myers, from behind Bloch, mouthed worriedly, I don't think he will.

Jansen seemed unperturbed by the double denial. "You will with practice. The stakes are high and worth a little trouble."

Myers said, "Go ahead, B.B. Just give it a read-through

and Mr. Jansen will help out as you go along.''

Bloch looked as though he wished to object further, but his native amiability won out. He put the manuscript on the lectern and began to read it. He stumbled, peered at the manuscript with a frown, began again, and skidded to a halt.

Jansen explained and Bloch began again. They spent an hour over the first three paragraphs before calling a halt.

Myers said, ''It's awful.''

Jansen said, ''How did you do the first time you tried to ride a bicycle?''

Bloch repeated the speech all the way through twice that day; twice more the second day. A second speech was prepared, not quite the same, but just as empty of real content.

After a week, Bloch said, ''I'm getting the hang of it. It seems to me that I'm getting so that it sounds good.''

Myers said, with hollow hopefulness, ''I think so, too.''

Jansen said to Myers afterward, ''He's doing better than I expected. He's got a certain potentiality, but—''

''But what?''

Jansen shrugged. ''Nothing. We'll just have to see.''

Jansen said, ''I think he's ready for an audience now, provided it's a homogenous one which we can analyze accurately.''

''The American Association of Textile Weavers needs a speaker and I think I can place B.B. with them. Can you handle that audience?''

''Weavers?'' said Jansen, thoughtfully. ''The economic position would be homogenous and I suspect the educational level would not be too wide a spread. I would need to have a breakdown on what city and states they represent and on the percentages coming from establishments of different size. Age, sex and the usual, too, of course.''

"I'll see what I can dig up from the Union, but there isn't much time, you know."

"We'll try to work quickly. We've got a great deal of the basics worked out. Your man is learning how to deliver a speech."

Myers laughed. "He's gotten to the point where he almost convinces *me*.—You know, I wouldn't want him in Congress. I would want him on television, selling my views—his, I mean—"

"Your views, you mean," said Jansen, dryly. "*He* has none."

"It doesn't matter. I'm counting my chickens—"

Bloch did well at the A.A.T.W. cocktail party. He followed his instructions, had smiled, had talked just a bit but not too much, had told a harmless joke or two and dropped a few names, and had, for the most part, done a lot of listening and nodding.

And yet Myers, from his table up front, felt a certain tightness. If B.B. flopped, they could try again, but if he flopped, would there be enough in him to make it worth his while to try again? This might be the test that would show that B.B. just didn't have it. What a waste, with that appearance! With that Roman senator head of his!

He stole a glance at Jansen, who sat at his left. The little man seemed utterly composed but there was a slight contraction of the eyebrows, as though there were a secret worry gnawing at him.

The dinner was over, the various business announcements were being made, the committee was being thanked, the people seated on the dais were being introduced—all the maddening details that seemed to be designed for no other purpose than to place additional unnecessary strain upon the speaker.

Myers stared earnestly at Bloch, caught his eye, and held up two fingers briefly. Go in and get them, B.B.!

Would he? The speech was an odd one, almost quixotic.

It would read oddly in the papers if it ever made the news columns, but it was full of button pushers—according to Jansen and his computer.

Bloch was standing up now. He stepped easily to the lectern and put the manuscript before him. He was always good at that; doing it slickly and unobtrusively so that the audience never really had it rubbed in their face that the speech was going to be read.

Myers thought, not entirely irrelevantly, of the time he had attended a meeting at which the speaker had somehow managed to knock off his manuscript with an over-energetic gesture. The manuscript could be picked up and rearranged but an audience died at that moment and could not be revived.

Bloch smiled at the audience and began slowly. (Don't wait too long to speed up, B.B.)

He didn't. He quickened the beat. At times, he stopped briefly to puzzle out a symbol but fortunately, that sounded like deliberation, the kind of thought you would expect of mature wisdom. It helped to have that appearance.

Then he spoke still more quickly and emotionally and, to Myers' surprise, he could feel the drumbeats start. There were those key phrases, with just the right kind of emphasis, and in response, he could feel the audience stir.

Laughter came on cue and at one point, there was a patter of applause. Myers had never heard applause interrupt Bloch before.

Bloch's face looked a little flushed and at one point he brought his fist down on the lectern and the little fluorescent lamp shook. (Don't knock it over, B.B.!) The audience stamped its feet in response.

Myers felt the mounting excitement within himself, even though he knew exactly how carefully the speech had been prepared. He leaned toward Jansen. "He's igniting the audience, wouldn't you say?"

Jansen nodded once. His lips scarcely moved. "Yes. And maybe—"

Bloch had paused briefly in his talk—just long enough to tighten the audience into a knot of tension—and then he brought his hand down savagely on the lectern, picked up the manuscript in a crumpled mess, and threw it aside. "I don't need this," he said, his voice rising into a distinct note of triumph. "I don't want it. I wrote it in cold blood before I had you all before me. Let me speak now from my heart, as it comes to me, standing here before you; let me tell you all, friends and Americans, you and I, together, what I see in the world today and what I *want* to see, and believe me, my friends, the two are *not—the—same.*"

There was a roar in response.

Myers clutched at Jansen wildly. "He can't make it on his own!"

But he could and did. He spoke through and over the applause and the shouting. It scarcely mattered if he were heard. He raised both arms as though to embrace the audience and a voice shouted, "Go on! Give it to them!"

Bloch gave it to them. Exactly what he said scarcely mattered but when it was over, there was a wild and jubilant standing ovation.

"What happened?" said Myers, through the noise. (He was applauding as loudly as everyone else.)

Jansen remained seated, in a strange attitude of collapse. He clutched at Myers, drew him close, and said in a shaking voice, "Don't you see what happened? It was a one-in-a-million shot. Just toward the end I began to wonder if it were possible. It *can* happen—"

"What are you talking about?"

"The audience ignited and Bloch was speaking to an ignited audience for the first time in his life, and speakers have their ignition point, too. Bloch himself ignited, and an ignited speaker can carry public opinion and move mountains."

"Who? B.B.?"

"Yes."

"Well, that's great."

"Is it? When ignited, he's got power, and if he finds out he has, why would he need you? Or me? And if so, where will he go? There have been great charismatics before who have not always led to glory."

Bloch was with them, people crowding about him. He said to Myers in a breathless undertone, "That was easy! I feel great!" He turned to those about him, laughing, holding them all with no trouble.

Myers looked after him, confused; Jansen looked after him, afraid!

LEST WE REMEMBER

1

The problem with John Heath, as far as John Heath was concerned, was that he struck a dead average. He was sure of it. What was worse, he felt that Susan suspected it.

It meant he would never make a true mark in the world, never climb to the top of Quantum Pharmaceuticals, where he was a steady cog among the junior executives—never make the Quantum Leap.

Nor would he do it anywhere else, if he changed jobs.

He sighed inwardly. In just two more weeks he was going to be married and for her sake he yearned to be upwardly mobile. After all, he loved her madly and wanted to shine in her eyes.

But then, that was dead average for a young man about to be married.

Susan Collins looked at John lovingly. And why not? He was reasonably good-looking and intelligent and a steady,

53

affectionate fellow besides. If he didn't blind her with his brilliance, he at least didn't upset her with an erraticism he didn't possess.

She patted the pillow she had placed behind his head when he sat down in the armchair and handed him his drink, making sure he had a firm grip before she let go.

She said, "I'm practicing to treat you well, Johnny. I've got to be an efficient wife."

John sipped at his drink. "I'm the one who'll have to be on my toes, Sue. Your salary is higher than mine."

"It's all going to go into one pocket once we're married. It will be the firm of Johnny and Sue keeping one set of books."

"You'll have to keep it," said John, despondently. "I'm bound to make mistakes if I try."

"Only because you're sure you will.—When are your friends coming?"

"Nine, I think. Maybe nine-thirty. And they're not exactly friends. They're Quantum people from the research labs."

"You're sure they won't expect to be fed?"

"They said after dinner. I'm positive about that. It's business."

She looked at him quizzically. "You didn't say that before."

"Say what before?"

"That it was business. Are you sure?"

John felt confused. Any effort to remember *precisely* always left him confused. "They said so—I think."

Susan's look was that of good-natured exasperation, rather like the one she would have given a friendly puppy who is completely unaware its paws are muddy. "If you really thought," she said, "as often as you say 'I think' you wouldn't be so perennially uncertain. Don't you see it *can't* be business. If it were business, wouldn't they see you *at* business?"

"It's confidential," said John. "They didn't want to see me at work. Not even at my apartment."

"Why here, then?"

"Oh, I suggested that. I thought you ought to be around, anyway. They're going to have to deal with the firm of Johnny and Sue, right?"

"It depends," said, Susan, "on what the confidential is all about. Did they give you any hints?"

"No, but it couldn't hurt to listen. It could be something that would give me a boost in standing at the firm."

"Why you?" asked Susan.

John looked hurt, "Why *not* me?"

"It just strikes me that someone at your job level doesn't require all that confidentiality and that—"

She broke off when the intercom buzzed. She dashed off to answer and came back to say, "They're on the way up."

2

Two of them were at the door. One was Boris Kupfer, whom John had already spoken to—large and restless, with a clear view of bluish stubble on his chin.

The other was David Anderson, smaller and more composed. His quick eyes moved this way and that, however, missing nothing.

"Susan," said John, uncertainly, still holding the door open. "These are the two colleagues of mine that I told you about. Boris—" He hit a blank in his memory banks and stopped.

"Boris Kupfer," said the larger man morosely, jingling some change in his pocket, "and David Anderson here. It's very kind of you, Miss—"

"Susan Collins."

"It's very kind of you to make your place of residence available to Mr. Heath and to us for a private conference. We apologize for trespassing on your time and your privacy in this manner—and if you could leave us to ourselves for a while, we will be further grateful.''

Susan stared at him solemnly. "Do you want me to go to the movies, or just into the next room?"

"If you could visit a friend—"

"No," said Susan, firmly.

"You can dispose of your time as you please, of course. A movie, if you wish."

"When I said 'No,'" said Susan, "I meant I wasn't leaving. I want to know what this is about."

Kupfer seemed nonplussed. He stared at Anderson for a moment, then said, "It's confidential, as Mr. Heath explained to you, I hope."

John, looking uneasy, said, "I explained that. Susan understands—"

"Susan," said Susan, "doesn't understand and wasn't given to understand that she was to absent herself from the proceedings. This is my apartment and Johnny and I are being married in two weeks—exactly two weeks from today. We are the firm of Johnny and Sue and you'll have to deal with the firm."

Anderson's voice sounded for the first time, surprisingly deep and as smooth as though it had been waxed. "Boris, the young woman is right. As Mr. Heath's soon-to-be wife, she will have a great interest in what we have come here to suggest and it would be wrong to exclude her. She has so firm an interest in our proposal that if she were to wish to leave, I would urge her most strongly to remain."

"Well, then, my friends," said Susan, "what will you have to drink? Once I bring you those drinks, we can begin."

Both were seated rather stiffly and had sipped cautiously at their drinks, and then Kupfer said, "Heath, I don't suppose you know much about the chemical details of the company's work—the cerebro-chemicals, for instance."

"Not a bit," said John, uneasily.

"No reason you should," said Anderson, silkily.

"It's like this," said Kupfer, casting an uneasy glance at Susan—

"No reason to go into technical details," said Anderson, almost at the lower level of audibility.

Kupfer colored slightly. "Without technical details, Quantum Pharmaceuticals deals with cerebro-chemicals which are, as the name implies, chemicals that affect the cerebrum; that is, the higher functioning of the brain."

"It must be very complicated work," said Susan, with composure.

"It is," said Kupfer. "The mammalian brain has hundreds of characteristic molecular varieties found no-where else, which serve to modulate cerebral activity, in-cluding aspects of what we might term the intellectual life. The work is under the closest corporate security, which is why Anderson wants no technical details. I *can* say this, though.—We can go no further with animal experiments. We're up against a brick wall if we can't try the human response."

"Then why don't you?" said Susan. "What stops you?"

"Public reaction if something goes wrong!"

"Use volunteers, then."

"That won't help. Quantum Pharmaceuticals couldn't take the adverse publicity if something went wrong."

Susan looked at them mockingly. "Are you two working on your own, then?"

Anderson raised his hand to stop Kupfer. "Young woman," he said, "let me explain briefly in order to put an end to wasteful verbal fencing. If we succeed, we will be enormously rewarded. If we fail, Quantum Pharma-ceuticals will disown us and we will pay what penalty there is to be paid, such as the ending of our careers. If you ask us, why we are willing to take this risk, the answer is, we do not think a risk exists. We are reasonably sure we will succeed; entirely sure we will do no harm. The corporation feels it cannot take the chance; but we feel we can.—Now, Kupfer, proceed!''

Kupfer said, ''We have a memory chemical. It works with every animal we have tried. Their learning ability improves amazingly. It should work on human beings, too.''

John said, ''That sounds exciting.''

''It *is* exciting,'' said Kupfer. ''Memory is not improved by devising a way for the brain to store information more efficiently. All our studies show that the brain stores almost unlimited numbers of items perfectly and permanently. The difficulty lies in recall. How many times have you had a name at the tip of your tongue and couldn't get it? How many times have you failed to come up with something you *knew* you knew, and then did come up with it two hours later when you were thinking about something else.—Am I putting it correctly, David?''

''You are,'' said Anderson. ''Recall is inhibited, we think, because the mammalian brain outraced its needs by developing a too-perfect recording system. A mammal stores more bits of information than it needs or is capable of using and if all of it was on tap at all times, it would never be able to choose among them quickly enough for appropriate reaction. Recall is inhibited, therefore, to insure that items emerge from memory storage in manipulable numbers, and with those items most desired not blurred by the accompaniment of numerous other items of no interest.

''There is a definite chemical in the brain that functions as a recall inhibitor, and we have a chemical that neutralizes the inhibitor. We call it a disinhibitor, and as far as we have been able to ascertain the matter, it has no deleterious side effects.''

Susan laughed. ''I see what's coming, Johnny. You can leave now, gentlemen. You just said that recall is inhibited to allow mammals to react more efficiently, and now you say that the disinhibitor has no deleterious side effects. Surely the disinhibitor will make the mammals react less efficiently; perhaps find themselves unable to react at all.

And now you are going to propose that you try it on Johnny and see if you reduce him to catatonic immobility or not.''

Anderson rose, his thin lips quivering. He took a few rapid strides to the far end of the room and back. When he sat down, he was composed and smiling. "In the first place, Miss Collins, it's a matter of dosage. We told you that the experimental animals all displayed enhanced learning ability. Naturally, we didn't eliminate the inhibitor entirely; we merely suppressed it in part. Secondly, we have reason to think the human brain *can* handle complete disinhibition. It is much larger than the brain of any animal we have tested and we all know its incomparable capacity for abstract thought.

"It is a brain designed for perfect recall, but the blind forces of evolution have not managed to remove the inhibiting chemical which, after all, was designed for and inherited from the lower animals.''

"Are you sure?" asked John.

"You *can't* be sure," said Susan, flatly.

Kupfer said, "We are sure, but we need the proof to convince others. That's why we have to try a human being.''

"John, in fact," said Susan.

"Yes.''

"Which brings us," said Susan, "to the key question. Why John?''

"Well," said Kupfer, slowly, "we need someone for whom chances of success are most nearly certain, and in whom it would be most demonstrable. We don't want someone so low in mental capacity that we must use dangerously large doses of the disinhibitor; nor do we want someone so bright that the effect will not be sufficiently noticeable. We need someone who's average. Fortunately, we have the full physical and psychological profiles of all the employees at Quantum and in this and, in fact, all other ways, Mr. Heath is ideal.''

"Dead average?" said Susan.

John looked stricken at the use of the phrase he had

thought his own innermost, and disgraceful, secret. "Come on, now." he said.

Ignoring John's outcry, Kupfer answered Susan, "Yes."

"And he won't be, if he submits to treatment?"

Anderson's lips stretched into another one of his cheerless smiles. "That's right. He won't be. This is something to think about if you're going to be married soon—the firm of Johnny and Sue, I think you called it. As it is, I don't think the firm will advance at Quantum, Miss Collins, for although Heath is a good and reliable employee he is, as you say, dead average. If he takes the disinhibitor, however, he will become a remarkable person and move upward with astonishing speed. Consider what that will mean to the firm."

"What does the firm have to lose?" asked Susan, grimly.

Anderson said, "I don't see how you can lose anything. It will be a sensible dose which can be administered at the laboratories tomorrow—Sunday. We will have the floor to ourselves; we will keep him under surveillance for a few hours.—It is certain nothing could go wrong. If I could tell you of our painstaking experimentation and of our thoroughgoing exploration of all possible side effects—"

"On animals," said Susan, not giving an inch.

But John said, tightly, "I'll make the decision, Sue. I've had it up to here with that dead-average bit. It's worth some risk to me if it means getting off that dead-average dead end."

"Johnny," said Susan, "don't jump."

"I'm thinking of the firm, Sue. I want to contribute my share."

Anderson said, "Good, but sleep on it. We will leave two copies of an agreement we will ask you to look over and sign. Please don't show it to anybody whether you sign or not. We will be here tomorrow morning again to take you to the laboratory."

They smiled, rose, and left.

John read over the agreement with a troubled frown, then

looked up. "You don't think I should be doing this, do you, Sue?"

"It worries me, sure."

"Look, if I have a chance to get away from that dead average—"

Susan said, "What's wrong with that? I've met so many nuts and cranks in my short life that I welcome a nice, average guy like you, Johnny. Listen, I'm dead average too."

"*You* dead average. With your looks? Your figure?"

Susan looked down upon herself with a touch of complacency. "Well, then, I'm just your dead-average gorgeous girl," she said.

3

The injection took place at 8 A.M. Sunday, no more than twelve hours after the proposition had been advanced. A thoroughly computerized body sensor was attached to John in a dozen places, while Susan watched with keen-eyed apprehension.

Kupfer said, "Please, Heath, relax. All is going well, but tension speeds the heart rate, raises the blood pressure, and skews our results."

"How can I relax?" muttered John.

Susan put in sharply, "Skews the results to the point where you don't know what's going on?"

"No, no," said Anderson. "Boris said all is going well and it is. It is just that our animals were always sedated before the injection, and we did not feel sedation would have been appropriate in this case. So if we can't have sedation, we must expect tension. Just breathe slowly and do your best to minimize it."

It was late afternoon before he was finally disconnected.

"How do you feel?" asked Anderson.

"Nervous," said John. "Otherwise, all right."

"No headache?"

"No. But I want to visit the bathroom. I can't exactly relax with a bedpan."

"Of course."

John emerged, frowning. "I don't notice any particular memory improvement."

"That will take some time and will be gradual. The disinhibitor must leak across the blood-brain barrier, you know," said Anderson.

4

It was nearly midnight when Susan broke what had turned out to be an oppressively silent evening in which neither had much responded to the television.

She said, "You'll have to stay here overnight. I don't want you alone when we don't really know what's going to happen."

"I don't feel a thing," said John, gloomily. "I'm still me."

"I'll settle for that, Johnny," said Susan. "Do you feel any pains or discomforts or oddnesses at all?"

"I don't think so."

"I wish we hadn't done it."

"For the firm," said John, smiling weakly. "We've got to take some chances for the firm."

5

John slept poorly, and woke drearily, but on time. And he arrived at work on time, too, to start the new week.

By 11 A.M., however, his morose air had attracted the unfavorable attention of his immediate superior, Michael Ross. Ross was burly and black-browed and fit the stereotype of the stevedore without being one. John got along with him though he did not like him.

Ross said, in his bass-baritone, "What's happened to your cheery disposition, Heath—your jokes—your lilting laughter?" Ross cultivated a certain preciosity of speech as though he were anxious to negate the stevedore image.

"Don't exactly feel tip-top," said John, not looking up.

"Hangover?"

"No, sir," said John, coldly.

"Well, cheer up, then. You'll win no friends, scattering stinkweeds over the fields as you gambol along."

John would have liked to groan. Ross's subliterary affectations were wearisome at the best of times and this wasn't the best of times.

And to make matters worse, John smelled the foul odor of a rancid cigar and knew that James Arnold Prescott— the head of the sales division—could not be far behind.

Nor was he. He looked about, and said, "Mike, when and what did we sell Rahway last spring or thereabouts? There's some damned question about it and I think the details have been miscomputerized."

The question was not addressed to him, but John said quietly, "Forty-two vials of PCAP. That was on April 14, J.P., invoice number P–20543, with a five per cent discount granted on payment within thirty days. Payment, in full, received on May 8."

Apparently everyone in the room had heard that. At least, everyone looked up.

Prescott said, "How the hell do you happen to know all that?"

John stared at Prescott for a moment, a vast surprise on his face. "I just happened to remember, J.P."

"You did, eh? Repeat it."

John did, faltering a bit, and Prescott wrote it down on one of the papers on John's desk, wheezing slightly as the bend at his waist compressed his portly abdomen up against his diaphragm and made breathing difficult. John tried to duck the smoke from the cigar without seeming to do so.

Prescott said, "Ross, check this out on your computer and see if there's anything to it at all." He turned to John with an aggrieved look. "I don't like practical jokers. What would you have done if I had accepted these figures of yours and walked off with them?"

"I wouldn't have done anything. They're correct," said John, conscious of himself as the full center of attention.

Ross handed Prescott the readout. Prescott looked at it and said, "This is from the computer?"

"Yes, J.P."

Prescott stared at it, then said, with a jerk of his head toward John, "And what's he? Another computer? His figures were correct."

John tried a weak smile, but Prescott growled and left, the stench of his cigar a lingering reminder of his presence.

Ross said, "What the hell was that little bit of legerdemain, Heath? You found out what he wanted to know and looked it up in advance to get some kudos?"

"No, sir," said John, who was gathering confidence. "I just happened to remember. I have a good memory for these things."

"And took the trouble to keep it from your loyal companions all these years? There's no one here who had any idea you hid a good memory behind that unremarkable forehead of yours."

"No point in showing it, Mr. Ross, is there? Now when I have, it doesn't seem to have gained me any goodwill, does it?"

And it hadn't. Ross glowered at him and turned away.

6

John's excitement over the dinner table at Gino's that night made it difficult for him to talk coherently, but Susan listened patiently and tried to act as a stabilizing force.

"You might just have happened to remember, you know," she said. "By itself it doesn't prove anything, Johnny."

"Are you crazy?" He lowered his voice at Susan's gesture and quick glance about. He repeated in a semiwhisper, "Are you crazy? You don't suppose it's the only thing I remember, do you? I think I can remember anything I ever heard. It's just a question of recall. For instance, quote some line out of Shakespeare."

"To be or not to be."

John looked scornful. "Don't be funny. Oh, well, it doesn't matter. The point is that if you recite any line, I can carry on from there for as long as you like. I read some of the plays for English Lit classes at college and some for myself and I can bring any of it back. I've tried. It flows! I suppose I can bring back any part of any book or article or newspaper I've ever read, or any TV show I've ever watched—word for word or scene for scene."

Susan said, "What will you do with all that?"

John said, "I don't have that consciously in my head at all times. Surely you don't—wait, let's order—"

Five minutes later, he said, "Surely you don't—My God, I haven't forgotten where we left off. Isn't it amazing?— Surely you don't think I'm swimming in a mental sea of Shakespearean sentences at all times. The recall takes an effort; not much of one, but an effort."

"How does it work?"

"I don't know. How do you lift your arm? What orders do you give your muscles? You just will the arm to lift upward and it does so. It's no trouble to do so, but your arm doesn't lift *until* you want it to. Well, I remember anything I've ever read or seen when I want to but not when I don't want to. I don't know how I do it, but I do it."

The first course arrived and John tackled it happily.

Susan picked at her stuffed mushrooms. "It sounds exciting."

"Exciting? I've got the biggest, most wonderful toy in

the world. **My own brain.** Listen, I can spell any word correctly and **I'm** pretty sure I won't ever make any grammatical mistake.''

"Because you remember all the dictionaries and grammars you ever read?"

John looked at her sharply. "Don't be sarcastic, Sue."

"I wasn't being—"

He waved her silent. "I never used dictionaries as light reading. But I do remember words and sentences in my reading and they were correctly spelled and correctly parsed."

"Don't be sure. You've seen any word misspelled in every possible way and every possible example of twisted grammar, too."

"Those were exceptions. By far the largest number of times I've encountered literary English, I've encountered it used correctly. It outweighs accidents, errors, and ignorance. What's more, I'm sure I'm improving even as I sit here, growing more intelligent steadily."

"And you're not worried. What if—"

"What if I become *too* intelligent? Tell me how on Earth you think becoming too intelligent can be harmful."

"I was going to say," said Susan, coldly, "that what you're experiencing is not intelligence. It's only total recall."

"How do you mean 'only'? If I recall perfectly, if I use the English language correctly, if I know endless quantities of material, isn't that going to make me seem more intelligent? How else need one define intelligence? You aren't growing just a little jealous, are you, Sue?"

"No," more coldly still. "I can always get an injection of my own if I feel desperate about it."

John put down his fork. "You can't mean that."

"I don't, but what if I did?"

"Because **you can't take** advantage of your special knowledge to **deprive me** of my position."

"What position?"

The main course arrived and for a few moments, John was busy. Then he said, in a whisper, "My position as the first of the future. *Homo superior!* There'll never be too many of us. You heard what Kupfer said. Some are too dumb to make it. Some are too smart to change much. I'm the one!"

"*Dead* average." One corner of Susan's mouth lifted.

"Once I was. There'll be others like me eventually. Not many, but there'll be others. It's just that I want to make my mark before the others come along. It's for the firm, you know. Us!"

He remained lost in thought thereafter, testing his brain delicately.

Susan ate in an unhappy silence.

7

John spent several days organizing his memories. It was like the preparation of an orderly reference book. One by one, he recalled all his experiences in the six years he had spent at Quantum Pharmaceuticals and all he had heard and all the papers and memos he had read.

There was no difficulty in discarding the irrelevant and unimportant and storing them in a "hold till further notice" compartment where they did not interfere with his analysis. Other items were put in order so that they established a natural progression.

Against that skeletal organization, he resurrected the scuttlebutt he had heard; the gossip, malicious or otherwise; casual phrases and interjections at conferences which he had not been conscious of hearing at the time. Those items which did not fit anywhere against the background he had built up in his head were worthless, empty of factual content. Those which did fit clicked firmly into place and could be seen as true by that mere fact.

The further the structure grew, and the more coherent, the more significant new items became and the easier it was to fit them in.

Ross stopped by John's desk on Thursday. He said, "I want to see you in my office at the nonce, Heath, if your legs will deign to carry you in that direction."

John rose uneasily. "Is it necessary? I'm busy."

"Yes, you look busy." Ross looked over the clear desk which, at the moment, held nothing but a studio photo of a smiling Susan. "You've been this busy all week. But you've asked me whether seeing me in my office is necessary. For me, no; but for you, vital. There's the door to my office. There's the door to the hell out of here. Choose one or the other and do it fast."

John nodded and, without undue hurry, followed Ross into his office.

Ross seated himself behind his desk but did not invite John to sit. He maintained a hard stare for a moment, then said, "What the hell's got into you this week, Heath. Don't you know what your job is?"

"To the extent that I have done it, it would seem that I do," said John. "The report on microcosmic is on your desk and complete and seven days ahead of deadline. I doubt that you can have complaints about it."

"You doubt, do you? Do I have permission to have complaints if I choose to after communing with my soul? Or am I condemned to applying to you for permission?"

"I apparently have not made myself plain, Mr. Ross. I doubt that you have *rational* complaints about it. To have those of the other variety is entirely up to you."

Ross rose now. "Listen, punk, if I decide to fire you, you won't get the news by word of mouth. It won't be anything I say that will give you the glad tidings. You will go out through the door in a violent tumble and mine will be the propulsive force behind that tumble. Just keep that in your small brain and your tongue in your big mouth.— Whether you've done your work or not is not at question

right now. Whether you've done everyone else's is. Who
and what gives you the right to manage everyone in this
place?''

John said nothing.

Ross roared, ''Well?''

John said, ''Your order was 'keep your tongue in your
big mouth.' ''

Ross turned a dangerous red. ''You will answer questions, however.''

John said, ''I am not aware that I have been managing
anyone.''

''There's not a person in the place you haven't corrected
at least once. You have gone over Willoughby's head in
connection with the correspondence on the TMP's; you have
been into general files using Bronstein's computer access;
and God knows what else I haven't yet been told about and
all in the last two days. You are disrupting the work of this
department and it must cease this moment. There must be
dead calm, and instantaneously, or it will be tornado weather
for you, my man.''

John said, ''If I have interfered in the narrow sense, it
has been for the good of the company. In the case of Willoughby, his treatment of the TMP matter was putting Quantum Pharmaceuticals in violation of government regulations,
something I have pointed out to you in one of several memos
I have sent you which you apparently have not had occasion
to read. As for Bronstein, he was simply ignoring general
directions and costing the company fifty thousand in unnecessary tests, something I was easily able to establish by
locating the necessary correspondence—merely to corroborate my clear memory of the situation.''

Ross was swelling visibly through the talk. ''Heath,'' he
said, ''you are usurping my role. You will, therefore, gather
. your personal effects and be off the premises before lunch,
never to return. If you do, I will take extreme pleasure in
helping you out again with my foot. Your official notice of
dismissal will be in your hands, or down your throat, before

your effects will be collected, work as quickly as you may."

John said, "Don't try to bully me, Ross. You've cost the company a quarter of a million dollars through incompetence and you know it."

There was a short pause as Ross deflated. He said, cautiously, "What are you talking about?"

"Quantum Pharmaceuticals went down to the wire on the Nutley bid and missed out because a certain piece of information that was in your hands stayed in your hands and never got to the Board of Directors. You either forgot or you didn't bother and in either case you are not the man for your job. You are either incompetent or have sold out."

"You're insane."

"No one need believe me. The information is in the computer, if one knows where to look and I know where to look. What's more, the knowledge is on file and will be on the desks of the interested parties two minutes after I leave these premises."

"If this were so," said Ross, speaking with difficulty, "you could not possibly know. This is a stupid attempt at blackmail by threat of slander."

"You know it's not slander. If you doubt that I have the information, let me tell you that there is one memorandum that is not in the records but can be reconstructed without too much difficulty from what is there. You would have to explain its absence and it will be presumed you have destroyed it. You know I'm not bluffing."

"It's still blackmail."

"Why? I'm making no demands and no threats. I'm merely explaining my actions of the past two days. Of course, if I'm forced to resign, I'll have to explain why I resigned, won't I?"

Ross said nothing.

John said, coolly, "Is my resignation being requested?"

"Get out of here!"

"With my job? Or without it?"

Ross said, "You have your job." His face was a study in hatred.

8

Susan had arranged a dinner at her apartment and had gone to considerable trouble for it. Never, in her own opinion, had she looked more enticing and never did she think it more important to move John, at least for a bit, away from his total concentration on his own mind.

She said, with an attempt at heartiness, "After all, we are celebrating the last nine days of single blessedness."

"We are celebrating more than that," said John with a grim smile. "It's only four days since I got the disinhibitor and already I've been able to put Ross in his place. He'll never bother me again."

"We each seem to have our own notion of sentiment," said Susan. "Tell me the details of *your* tender remembrance."

John told the tale crisply, repeating the conversation verbatim and without hesitation.

Susan listened stonily, without in any way rising to the gathering triumph in John's voice. "How *did* you know all that about Ross?"

John said, "There are no secrets, Sue. Things just *seem* secret because people don't remember. If you can recall every remark, every comment, every stray word made to you or in your hearing and consider them all in combination, you find that everyone gives himself away in everything. You can pick out meanings that will, in these days of computerization, send you straight to the necessary records. It can be done. I can do it. I have done it in the case of Ross. I can do it in the case of anybody with whom I associate."

"You can also get them furious."

"I got Ross furious. You can bet on that."

"Was that wise?"

"What can he do to me? I've got him cold."

"He has enough clout in the upper echelons—"

"Not for long. I have a conference set for 2 P.M. tomorrow with old man Prescott and his stinking cigar and I'll cut Ross off at the pass."

"Don't you think you're moving too quickly?"

"Moving too quickly? I haven't even begun. Prescott's just a stepping-stone. Quantum Pharmaceutical's just a stepping-stone."

"It's still too quick. Johnny, you need someone to direct you. You need—"

"I need *nothing*. With what I have," he tapped his temple, "there's no one and nothing that can stop me."

Susan said, "Well, look, let's not discuss that. We have different plans to make."

"Plans?"

"Our own. We're getting married in just under nine days. Surely," with heavy irony, "you haven't returned to the sad old days when you forgot things."

"I remember the wedding," said John, testily, "but at the moment I've got to reorganize Quantum. In fact, I've been thinking seriously of postponing the wedding till I have things well in hand."

"Oh? And when might that be?"

"That's hard to tell. Not long at the rate I'm taking hold. A month or two, I suppose. Unless," and he descended into sarcasm, "you think that's moving too quickly."

Susan was breathing hard. "Were you planning to consult with me on the matter?"

John raised his eyebrows. "Would it have been necessary? Where's the argument? Surely you see what's happening. We can't interrupt it and lose momentum.—Listen, did you know I'm a mathematical wiz. I can multiply and divide as fast as a computer because at some time in my life I have come across almost every simple bit of arithmetic and I can *recall* the answers. I read a table of square roots and I can—"

Susan cried, "My God, Johnny, you *are* a kid with a new toy. You've lost your perspective. Instant recall is good for nothing but playing tricks with. It doesn't give you one bit more intelligence; not an ounce; not a speck more of judgment; not a whiff more of common sense. You're about as safe to have around as a little boy with a loaded grenade. You need looking after by someone with brains."

John scowled. "Do I? It seems to me that I'm getting what I want."

"Are you? Isn't it true that I'm what you want also?"

"What?"

"Go ahead, Johnny. You want me. Reach out and take me. Exercise that remarkable recall you have. Remember who I am, what I am, the things we can do, the warmth, the affection, the sentiment."

John, with his forehead still creased in uncertainty, extended his arms toward Susan.

She stepped out of them. "But you haven't got me, or anything about me. You can't remember me into your arms; you have to love me into them. The trouble is, you don't have the good sense to do it and you lack the intelligence to establish reasonable priorities.—Here, take this and get out of my apartment or I'll hit you with something a lot heavier."

He stopped to pick up the engagement ring. "Susan—"

"I said, get out. The firm of Johnny and Sue is hereby dissolved."

Her face blazed anger and John turned meekly and left.

9

When he arrived at Quantum the next morning, Anderson was waiting for him with a look of anxious impatience on his face.

"Mr. Heath," he said, smiling, and rising.

"What do you want?" demanded John.

"We are private here, I take it?"

"The place isn't bugged as far as I know."

"You are to report to us day after tomorrow for examination. On Sunday. You recall that?"

"Of course, I recall that. I'm incapable of not recalling. I *am* capable of changing my mind, however. Why do I need an examination?"

"Why not, sir? It is quite plain from what Kupfer and I have picked up that the treatment seems to have worked splendidly. Actually, we don't want to wait till Sunday. If you can come with me today—now, in fact—it would mean a great deal to us, to Quantum, and, of course, to humanity."

John said, curtly, "You might have held on to me when you had me. You sent me about my business, allowing me to live and work unsupervised so that you could test me under field conditions, and get a better idea of how things would work out. It meant more risk for me, but you didn't worry about that, did you?"

"Mr. Heath, that was not in our minds. We—"

"Don't tell me that. I remember every last word you and Kupfer said to me last Sunday, and it's quite clear to me that that *was* in your minds. So if I take the risk, I accept the benefits. I have no intention of presenting myself as a biochemical freak who has achieved my ability at the end of a hypodermic needle. Nor do I want others of the sort wandering around. For now, I have a monopoly and I intend to use it. When I'm ready—not before—I will be willing to cooperate with you and benefit humanity. But just remember, I'm the one who will know when I'm ready, not you. So don't call me; I'll call you."

Anderson managed a soft smile. "As to that, Mr. Heath, how can you stop us from making our announcement? Those who have dealt with you this week will have no trouble in recognizing the change in you and in testifying to it."

"Really? See here, Anderson, listen closely and do so

without that foolish grin on your face. It irritates me. I told
you I remember every word you and Kupfer spoke. I remember every nuance of expression, every sidelong glance.
It all spoke volumes. I learned enough to check through
sick-leave records with a good idea of what I was looking
for. It would seem that I was not the first Quantum employee
on whom you had tried the disinhibitor.''

Anderson was, indeed, not smiling. ''That is nonsense.''

''You know it is not, and you had better know I can prove
it. I know the names of the men involved—one was a
woman, actually—and the hospitals in which they were
treated and the false history with which they were supplied.
Since you did not warn me of this, when you used me as
your fourth experimental animal on two legs, I owe you
nothing but a prison sentence.''

Anderson said, ''I won't discuss this matter. Let me say
this, though. The treatment will wear off, Heath. You won't
keep your total recall. You will have to come back for further
treatment and you can be sure it will be on our terms.''

John said, ''Nuts! You don't suppose I haven't investi-
gated your reports—at least, those you haven't kept secret.
And I already have a notion of what aspects you *have* kept
secret. The treatment lasts longer in some cases than others.
It invariably lasts longer where it is more effective. In my
case, the treatment has been extraordinarily effective and it
will endure a considerable time. By the time I come to you
again, if I ever have to, I will be in a position where any
failure on your part to cooperate will be swiftly devastating
to you. Don't even think of it.''

''You ungrateful—''

''Don't bother me,'' said John, wearily. ''I have no time
to listen to you froth. Go away, I have work to do.''

Anderson's face was a study in fear and frustration as he
left.

10

It was 2:30 P.M. when John walked into Prescott's office, for once not minding the cigar smoke. It would not be long, he knew, before Prescott would have to choose between his cigars and his position.

With Prescott were Arnold Gluck and Lewis Randall, so that John had the grim pleasure of knowing he was facing the three top men in the division.

Prescott rested his cigar on top of an ashtray and said, "Ross has asked me to give you half an hour, and that's all I will give you. You're the one with the trick memory, aren't you?"

"My name is John Heath, sir, and I intend to present you with a rationalization of procedure for the company; one that will make full use of the age of computers and electronic communication and will lay the groundwork for further modification as the technology improves."

The three men looked at each other.

Gluck, whose creased face was tanned a leathery-brown, said, "Are you an expert in office management?"

"I don't have to be, sir. I have been here for six years and I recall every bit of the procedure in every transaction in which I have been involved. That means the pattern of such transactions is plain to me and its imperfections obvious. One can see toward what it is tending and where it is doing so wastefully and inefficiently. If you'll listen, I will explain. You will find it easy to understand."

Randall, whose red hair and freckles made him seem younger than he was, said sardonically, "Real easy, I hope, because we have trouble with hard concepts."

"You won't have trouble," said John.

"And you won't get a second more than twenty-one minutes," said Prescott, looking at his watch.

"It won't take that," said John. "I have it diagrammed and I can talk quickly."

It took fifteen minutes and the three management personnel were remarkably silent in that interval.

Finally Gluck said, with a hostile glance out of his small eyes, "It sounds as though you are saying we can get along with half the management we are employing these days."

"Less than half," said John, coolly, "and be the more efficient for it. We can't fire ordinary personnel at will because of the unions, though we can profitably lose them by attrition. Management is not protected, however, and can be let go. They'll have pensions if they're old enough and can get new jobs if they're young enough. Our thought must be for Quantum."

Prescott, who had maintained an ominous silence, now puffed furiously at his noxious cigar and said, "Changes like this have to be considered carefully and implemented, if at all, with the greatest of caution. What seems logical on paper can lose out in the human equation."

John said, "Prescott, if this reorganization is not accepted within a week, and if I am not placed in charge of its implementation, I will resign. I will have no trouble in finding employment with a smaller firm where this plan can be far more easily put into practice. Beginning with a small group of management people, I can expand in both quantity and efficiency of performance without additional hiring and within a year I'll drive Quantum into bankruptcy. It would be fun to do this if I am driven to it, so consider carefully. My half hour is up. Good-bye." And he left.

11

Prescott looked after him with a glance of frigid calculation. He said to the other two, "I think he means what he says and that he knows every facet of our operations better than we do. We can't let him go."

"You mean we've got to accept his plan," said Randall, shocked.

"I didn't say that. You two go, and remember this whole thing is confidential."

Gluck said, "I have the feeling that if we don't do something, all three of us will find ourselves on our butts in the street within a month."

"Very likely," said Prescott, "so we'll do something."

"What?"

"If you don't know, you won't get hurt. Leave it to me. Forget it for now and have a nice weekend."

When they were gone, he thought a while, chewing furiously on his cigar. He then turned to his telephone and dialed an extension. "Prescott here. I want you in my office first thing Monday morning. First thing. Hear me?"

12

Anderson looked a trifle disheveled. He had had a bad weekend. Prescott, who had had a worse, said to him, malevolently, "You and Kupfer tried again, didn't you?"

Anderson said, softly, "It's better not to discuss that, Mr. Prescott. You remember it was agreed that in certain aspects of research, a distance was to be established. We were to take the risks or the glory, and Quantum was to share in the latter but not in the former."

"And your salary was doubled with a guarantee of all legal payments to be Quantum's responsibility; don't forget that. This man, John Heath, was treated by you and Kupfer, wasn't he? Come on. There's no mistaking it. There's no point in hiding it."

"Well, yes."

"And you were so brilliant that you turned him loose on us—this—this—tarantula."

"We didn't anticipate this would happen. When he didn't go into instant shock, we thought it was our first chance to test the process in the field. We thought he would break down after two or three days, or it would pass."

Prescott said, "If I hadn't been protected so damned well, I wouldn't have put the whole thing out of my mind and I would have guessed what had happened when that bastard first pulled the computer bit and produced the details of correspondence he had no business remembering.—All right, we know where we are now. He's holding the company to ransom with a new plan of operations he can't be allowed to put through. Also, he can't be allowed to walk away from us."

Anderson said, "Considering Heath's capacity for recall and synthesis, is it possible that his plan of operations may be a good one?"

"I don't care if it is. That bastard is after my job and who knows what else and we've got to get rid of him."

"How do you mean, rid of him? He could be of vital importance to the cerebrochemical project."

"Forget that. It's a disaster. You're creating a super-Hitler."

Anderson said, in soft-voiced anguish, "The effect will wear off."

"Yes? When?"

"At this moment, I can't be sure."

"Then I can't take chances. We've got to make our arrangements and do it tomorrow at the latest. We can't wait any longer."

13

John was in high good humor. The manner in which Ross avoided him when he could and spoke to him deferentially when he had to affected the entire work force. There was a strange and radical change in the pecking order, with himself at the top.

Nor could John deny to himself that he liked it. He reveled in it. The tide was moving strongly and unbelievably swiftly.

It was only nine days since the injection of the disinhibitor and every step had been forward.

Well, no, there had been Susan's silly rage at him, but he would deal with her later. When he showed her the heights to which he would climb in nine additional days—in ninety—

He looked up. Ross was at his desk, waiting for his attention but reluctant to do anything as crass as to attract that attention by as much as clearing his throat. John swiveled his chair, put his feet out before him in an attitude of relaxation, and said, "Well, Ross?"

Ross said, carefully, "I would like to see you in my office, Heath. Something important has come up and, frankly, you're the only one who can set it straight."

John got slowly to his feet. "Yes? What is it?"

Ross looked about mutely at the busy room, with at least five men in reasonable earshot. Then he looked toward his office door and held out an inviting arm.

John hesitated, but for years Ross had held unquestioned authority over him, and at this moment he reacted to habit.

Ross held his door open for John politely, stepped through himself and closed the door behind him, locking it unobtrusively and remaining in front of it. Anderson stepped out from the other side of the bookcase.

John said sharply, "What's all this about?"

"Nothing at all, Heath," said Ross, his smile turning into a vulpine grin. "We're just going to help you out of your abnormal state—take you back to normality. Don't move, Heath."

Anderson had a hypodermic in his hand. "Please, Heath, do not struggle. We wish you no harm."

"If I yell—" said John.

"If you make any sound," said Ross, "I will put a hammerlock on you and hold it till your eyes bug out. I would like to do that, so please try to yell."

John said, "I have the goods on both of you, safe on deposit. Anything that happens to me—"

"Mr. Heath," said Anderson, "nothing will happen to you. Something is going to *un*happen to you. We will put you back to where you were. That would happen anyway, but we will hurry it up just a little."

"So I'm going to hold you, Heath," said Ross, "and you won't move because if you do, you will disturb our friend with the needle and he might slip and give you more than the carefully calculated dose, and you might end up unable to remember anything at all."

Heath was backing away, breathless. "That's what you're planning. You think you'll be safe that way. If I forgot all about you, all about the information, all about its storage. But—"

"We're not going to hurt you, Heath," said Anderson.

John's forehead glistened with sweat. A near-paralysis gripped him.

"An amnesiac!" he said, huskily, and with a terror that only someone could feel at the possibility who himself had perfect recall.

"Then you won't remember this either, will you?" said Ross. "Go ahead, Anderson."

"Well," muttered Anderson, in resignation. "I'm destroying a perfect test-subject." He lifted John's flaccid arm and readied the hypodermic.

There was a knock at the door. A clear voice called, "John!"

Anderson froze almost automatically, looking up questioningly.

Ross had turned to look at the door. Now he turned back. "Shoot that stuff into him, doc," he said in an urgent whisper.

The voice came again, "Johnny, I know you're in there. I've called the police. They're on the way."

Ross whispered again, "Go ahead. She's lying. And by the time they come, it's over. Who can prove anything?"

But Anderson was shaking his head vigorously. "It's his

fiancée. She knows he was treated. She was there.''

"You jackass."

There was the sound of a kick against the door and then the voice sounded in a muffled, "Let go of me. They've got—Let go!"

Anderson said, "Having her push the thing was the only way we could get him to agree. Besides, I don't think we have to do anything. Look at him."

John had collapsed in a corner, eyes glazed, and clearly in a state of unconscious trance.

Anderson said, "He's been terrified and that can produce a shock that will interfere with recall under normal conditions. I think the disinhibitor has been wiped out. Let her in and let *me* talk to her."

14

Susan looked pale as she sat with her arm protectively about the shoulders of her ex-fiancé. "What happened?"

"You remember the injection of—"

"Yes, yes. What happened?"

"He was supposed to come to our office day before yesterday, Sunday, for a thorough examination. He didn't come. We worried and the reports from his superiors had me very perturbed. He was becoming arrogant, megalomaniacal, irascible—Perhaps you noticed.—You're not wearing your engagement ring."

"We—quarreled," said Susan.

"Then you understand. He was—Well, if he were an inanimate device, we might say his motor was overheating as it sped faster and faster. This morning it seemed absolutely essential to treat him. We persuaded him to come here, locked the door and—"

"Injected him with something while I howled and kicked outside."

"Not at all," said Anderson. "We would have used a

sedative, but we were too late. He had what I can only describe as a breakdown. You may search his body for fresh punctures, which, as his fiancée, I presume you may do without embarrassment, and you will find none."

Susan said, "I'll see about that. What happens, now?"

"I am sure he will recover. He will be his old self again."

"Dead average?"

"He will not have perfect recall, but until ten days ago, he never had.—Naturally, the firm will give him indefinite leave on full salary. If any medical treatment is required, all medical expenses will be paid. And when he feels like it, he can return to active duty."

"Yes? Well, I will want all that in writing before the day is out, or I see my lawyer tomorrow."

"But Miss Collins," said Anderson, "you know that Mr. Heath volunteered. You were willing too."

"I think," said Susan, "that *you* know the situation was misrepresented to us and that you won't welcome an investigation. Just see to it that what you've just promised is in writing."

"You will have to, in return, sign an agreement to hold us guiltless of any misadventure your fiancé may have suffered."

"Possibly. I prefer to see what kind of misadventure it is first.—Can you walk, Johnny?"

John nodded and said, a little huskily, "Yes, Sue."

"Then let's go."

15

John had put himself outside a cup of good coffee and an omelet before Susan permitted discussion. Then he said, "What I don't understand is how you happened to be there?"

"Shall we say woman's intuition?"

"Let's say Susan's brains."

"All right. Let's! After I threw the ring at you, I felt self-pitying and aggrieved and after that wore off, I felt a severe sense of loss because, odd though it might seem to the average sensible person, I'm very fond of you."

"I'm sorry, Sue," said John, humbly.

"As well you should be. God, you were insupportable. But then I got to thinking that if you could get poor loving me that furious, what must you be doing to your co-workers. The more I thought about it, the more I thought they might have a strong impulse to kill you. Now, don't get me wrong. I'm willing to admit you deserved killing, but only at *my* hands. I wouldn't dream of allowing anyone else to do it. I didn't hear from you—"

"I know, Sue. I had plans and I had no time—"

"You had to do it all in two weeks. I know, you idiot. By this morning I couldn't stand it anymore. I came to see how you were and found you behind a locked door."

John shuddered. "I never thought I'd welcome your kicking and screaming, but I did then. You stopped them."

"Will it upset you to talk about it?"

"I don't think so. I'm all right."

"Then what were they doing?"

"They were going to re-inhibit me. I thought they might be giving me an overdose and make me an amnesiac."

"Why?"

"Because they knew I had them all. I could ruin them and the company."

"You really could."

"Absolutely."

"But they didn't actually inject you, did they? Or was that another of Anderson's lies?"

"They really didn't."

"Are you all right?"

"I'm not an amnesiac."

"Well, I hate to sound like a Victorian damsel, but I hope you have learned your lesson."

"If you mean, do I realize you were right, I do."

"Then just let me lecture you for one minute, so you don't forget again. You went about everything too rapidly, too openly, and with too much disregard for the possible violent counteraction of others. You had total recall and you mistook it for intelligence. If you had someone who was really intelligent to guide you—"

"I needed you, Sue."

"Well, you've got me now, Johnny."

"What do we do next, Sue?"

"First, we get that paper from Quantum and, since you're all right, we'll sign the release for them. Second, we get married on Saturday, just as we originally planned. Third, we'll see—But, Johnny?"

"Yes?"

"You're all right?"

"Couldn't be better, Sue. Now we're together, everything's fine."

16

It wasn't a formal wedding. Less formal than they had originally planned and fewer guests. No one was there from Quantum, for instance—Susan had pointed out, quite firmly, that that would be a bad idea.

A neighbor of Susan's had brought a video-camera to record the proceedings, something that seemed to John to be the height of schlock, but Susan had wanted it.

And then the neighbor had said to him with a tragic shrug, "Can't get the damn thing to turn on. You'd think they'd give me one in working order. I'll have to make a phone call." He hastened down the steps to the pay phone in the chapel lobby.

John advanced to look at the camera curiously. An instruction booklet lay on a small table to one side. He picked it up and leafed through the pages with moderate speed, then put it back. He looked about him, but everyone was busy. No one seemed to be paying attention to him.

He slid the rear panel to one side, unobtrusively, and peered inside. He then turned away and gazed at the opposite wall thoughtfully. He was still gazing even as his right hand snaked in toward the mechanism and made a quick adjustment. After a brief interval he put the rear panel back and flicked to toggle switch.

The neighbor came bustling back, looking exasperated. "How am I going to follow directions I can't make head or—" He frowned, then said, "Funny. It's on. It must have been working all the time."

17

"You may kiss the bride," said the minister, benignly, and John took Susan in his arms and followed orders with enthusiasm.

Susan whispered through unmoving lips, "You fixed that camera. Why?"

He whispered back, "I wanted everything right for the wedding."

She whispered, "You wanted to show off."

They broke apart, looking at each other through love-misted eyes, then fell into another embrace, while the small audience stirred and tittered.

Susan whispered, "You do it again, and I'll skin you. As long as no one knows you still have it, no one will stop you. We'll have it all within a year, if you follow directions."

"Yes, dear," whispered John, humbly.

SAVING HUMANITY

My friend, George, sighing lugubriously, said to me, one evening, "I have a friend who is a klutz."

I nodded wisely. "Birds of a feather," I said.

George gazed at me in astonishment. "What have feathers to do with it? You have the most remarkable ability to skid away from a subject. It is the result, I suppose, of your thoroughly inadequate intellect—which I mention in pity, and not as reproof."

"Well, well," I said, "let that be as it may. When you refer to your friend the klutz, are you speaking of Azazel?"

Azazel was the two-centimeter demon or extraterrestrial being (take your pick) concerning whom George talks about constantly, ceasing only in response to a direct question. Freezingly, he said, "Azazel is not a subject for conversation, and I do not understand how you came to have heard of him."

"I happened to be within a mile of you one day," I said. George paid no attention, but said:

I first came across the uneuphonious word "klutz," in fact, through a conversation with my friend, Menander Block. You have never met him, I'm afraid, for he is a University man and therefore rather selective in his friendships, for which one, observing you, can scarcely blame him.

The word, klutz, he told me, referred to an awkward, clumsy person. "And that's me," he said. "It comes from a Yiddish word that, taken literally, means a piece of wood, a log, a block; and, of course, my name, as you will note, is Block."

He heaved an enormous sigh. "And yet I am not a klutz in the strict meaning of the word. There is nothing wooden, loggish or blockish about me. I dance as lightly as a zephyr and as gracefully as a dragonfly; I am sylph-like in every motion; and numerous young women could testify, if I thought it safe to allow them to do so, of my skill as a disciple of the amatory art. It is, rather, that I am a klutz at long distance. Without being myself affected, everything about me becomes klutzish. The very Universe itself seems to trip over its own cosmic feet. I suppose if you want to mix languages and combine Greek with Yiddish, I am a 'teleklutz'."

"How long has this been going on, Menander?" I asked.

"All my life, but, of course, it was only as an adult that I realized this peculiar quality I possess. While still a youth, I simply assumed that what happened to me was the normal state of affairs."

"Have you discussed this with anyone?"

"Of course not, George, old fellow. I would be considered mad. Can you see a psychoanalyst, for instance, confronting the phenomenon of teleklutzism. He would have me in the funny house half way through my first session and write a paper on his discovery of a new psychosis and probably become a millionaire as a result. I'm not going to the booby hatch just to enrich some psychomedical leech. I cannot tell *anyone* this."

"Then why are you telling me this, Menander?"

"Because, on the other hand, it seems to me I must tell someone if I am to remain functional. As it happens, you are the least someone I know."

I did not follow his reasoning there, but I could see that I was about to be subjected once again to the unwanted confidences of my friends. It was the price, I well knew, of the fact that I was proverbial for my understanding, sympathy, and most of all, for my close-mouthed reticence. No secret placed in my keeping would ever reach the ears of anyone else.—I make an exception in your case, of course, since it is well-known that you have an attention span of five seconds, and a memory-span of rather less.

I signalled for another drink and indicated, by a certain arcane sign that I alone know, that it was to be placed on Menander's tab. A laborer, after all, is worthy of his hire. I said, "Just how does this teleklutzism manifest itself, Menander?"

"In its simplest form, and in the manner that was first brought to my attention, it shows up in the peculiar weather that accompanies my travels. I do not travel very much, and when I do, I go by car, and when I do *that*, it rains. It doesn't matter what the weather forecast is; it doesn't matter how brightly the sun is shining when I start out. The clouds gather, grow darker and it begins to drizzle and then to pour. When my teleklutzism is in particular fettle, the temperature drops and we have an ice-storm.

"Of course, I am careful not to be foolish. I refuse to drive into New England until March is safely over. Last spring, I drove to Boston on April 6—which promptly had the first April blizzard in the history of the Boston Weather Bureau. I once drove to Williamsburg, Virginia, on March 28, assuming that I might be allowed a few days of grace considering that I was penetrating Dixie. Hah! Williamsburg had nine inches of snow that day and the natives were trying to rub some of it between their fingers and were asking each other what the white stuff was.

"I have often thought that if we imagined the Universe to be under the personal direction of God, we might picture Gabriel rushing into the divine presence to cry out, 'Holy One, two galaxies are about to collide in an unimaginably enormous catastrophe', and God would answer, 'Don't bother me now, Gabriel; I'm busy making it rain on Menander.' "

I said, "You might make the best of the situation, Menander? Why not sell your services, for fabulous sums, as a drought-breaker?"

"I have thought of that, but the mere thought dries up any rain that might occur during my travels. Besides, if the rain came when it was needed, it would probably produce a flood.

"And it's not only rain, or traffic jams, or the disappearance of landmarks; there are myriads of other things. Expensive objects break spontaneously in my presence, or are dropped by others through no fault attributable to myself. There is an advanced particle accelerator in operation in Batavia, Illinois. One day an enormously important experiment was ruined because of the failure of its vacuum; a completely unexplained failure. Only I knew (the next day, that is, when I read of the incident in the paper) that at the very moment of failure, I happened to be passing the outskirts of Batavia in a bus. It was raining, of course.

"At this very moment, old fellow, some of the fine five-day-old wine in the cellars of this fine establishment, being aged in the plastic, is turning sour. Someone brushing past this table at this moment will, when he arrives home, find that the pipes in his cellar have burst at the precise moment he passed me; except that he won't know that he passed me at that precise moment and that the passage was the cause. And so it will be with myriads of accidents; supposed accidents, that is."

My heart bled for my young friend. And my blood froze at the thought that I was sitting next to him and that at my cozy digs unimaginable catastrophes might be taking place.

I said, "You are, in short, a jinx!"

Menander threw his head back and stared down his nose at me in a most unpleasant way. "Jinx," he said, "is the common term; teleklutz is the scientific one."

"Well, then, jinx or teleklutz, suppose I told you I could perhaps remove this curse from you?"

"Curse is right," Menander said, gloomily. "I have often thought that, at the time of my birth, an ill-natured fairy, irked at not having been invited to the christening—Are you trying to tell me you can cancel curses because you are a good fairy?"

"I am not any kind of fairy," I said severely. "Just suppose I can remove this cur—condition of yours."

"How on Earth could you do that?"

"Not exactly on Earth," I said. "But how about it?"

"What do *you* get out of it?" he asked, suspiciously.

"The heart-warming feeling of having helped save a friend from a horrible life."

Menander thought about it and then shook his head firmly. "That's not enough."

"Of course, if you want to offer me some small sum—"

"No, no. I wouldn't think of insulting you that way. Offer a sum of money to a *friend*? Place a fiscal value on friendship? How could you think that of me, George? What I meant was that removing my teleklutzism isn't enough. You must do more than that."

"How can one do more?"

"Consider! Through my life I have been responsible for anything from inconvenience to catastrophe to perhaps millions of innocent people. Even if I brought no ill-fortune to a single person from this moment on, the evil I have done thus far—even though none of it was voluntary or in any way to be considered my fault—is more than I can bear. I must have something that will cancel it all out."

"Like what?"

"I must be in a position to save humanity."

"Save humanity?"

"What else can possibly balance the immeasurable damage I have done? George, I insist. If you are going to remove my curse, replace it with the ability to save humanity in some great crisis."

"I'm not sure that I can."

"*Try*, George. Don't shy away at this crisis. If you're going to do a job, do it well, I always say. Think of humanity, old friend."

"Wait a moment," I said, alarmed, "you're putting this whole thing on my shoulders."

"Of course I am, George," Menander said, warmly. "Broad shoulders! Good shoulders! Made to bear burdens! Go home, George, and arrange to remove this curse from me. A grateful humanity will shower you with blessings except, of course, that they will never hear of it, for I will tell no one. Your good deeds are not be be shamed by exposure, and rely on me, I will never expose them."

There is something wonderful about unselfish friendship that can be duplicated by nothing else on Earth. I rose at once to get to my task and left so quickly that I neglected to pay my half of the dinner bill. Fortunately, Menander did not notice this till I was safely out of the restaurant.

I had some trouble getting in touch with Azazel and in opening the hyperdimensional gateway between his world and ours. Nor did he seem good-natured about it at all. His two-centimeter-tall body was wrapped in a pinkish glow and, in his piping voice, he said, "Has it occurred to you that I might be showering?"

And indeed there was a very faint smell of ammonia about him.

I said, humbly, "This is a rather enormous emergency, oh Mighty-One-For-Whom-Words-Are-Insufficient."

"Well then, tell me, but mind, don't take all day about it."

"Certainly!" I said, and outlined the matter with admirable conciseness.

"Hmm," said Azazel. "For once you have presented me with an interesting problem."

"I have? Do you mean there is indeed such a thing as teleklutzism."

"Oh, yes. It is common on my world and is usually removed by inoculation during childhood. You see quantum mechanics makes it quite clear that the properties of the Universe depend, to a certain extent, on the observer. Just as the Universe affects the observer, the observer affects the Universe. Some observers affect the Universe adversely, or at least adversely with respect to some other observers. Thus, one observer may accelerate the supernovadom of some star, which would irritate other observers who may find themselves uncomfortably close to that star at the time."

"I see. Well, can you inoculate my friend, Menander, and remove this quantum-observational effect of his?"

"Oh, of course! Simple! It will take ten seconds and then I can return to my shower and to the rite of laskorati I will undertake with two samini of unimaginable loveliness."

"Wait! Wait! That's not enough."

"Don't be silly. Two samini are *quite* enough. Only a lecher would want three."

"I mean removing the teleklutzism isn't enough. Menander also wants to be in a position to save humanity."

For a minute, I thought Azazel was going to forget our long friendship and all I had done for him in the way of supplying him with interesting problems that probably improved his mind and his scientific abilities. I did not understand all he said, for most of the words were in his own language but they sounded very much like saws scrapping along rusty nails.

Finally, having cooled down to a dim red-heat, he said, "Now how am I going to do that?"

"Is anything too much for the Apostle-of-Incredibility?"

"You bet!—But let's see!" He thought for a while, and burst out, "But who in the Universe would *want* to save humanity? Where's the worth in doing that? You stink up this whole section—Well, well, I think it can be done."

It didn't take ten seconds. It took half an hour and a very uncomfortable half-hour it was, too, with Azazel groaning part of the time and the rest of the time stopping to wonder if the samini were going to wait for him.

He was done eventually and, or course, it meant I would have to test out the matter on Menander Block.

When I next saw Menander, I said, "You're cured."

He stared at me hostilely, "Do you know that you stuck me with the dinner check the other night?"

"Surely a minor point compared with the fact that you're cured."

"I don't feel cured."

"Well, come. Let's take a drive together. You take the wheel."

"It looks cloudy already. Some cure!"

"Drive! What have we to lose?"

He backed the car out of his garage. A man passing by on the other side of the street did not trip over an overloaded garbage can.

He drove down the street. The light did not turn red as he approached, and two cars skidding toward each other at the intersection next but one, missed each other by a comfortable margin.

By the time he was at the bridge, the clouds had thinned out and a warm sun was shining down upon the car. It was not in his eyes.

When we finally got home, he was weeping unashamedly, and I parked the car for him. I scraped it slightly, but it was not *I* that had had my teleklutzism cured. At that, it might have been worse. I might have scraped my own car.

For the next few days, he was seeking me out constantly.

I was the only one, after all, who could understand the miracle that had taken place.

He would say, "I went to a dance, and not one couple tripped over each other's feet and fell down and broke a collar bone or two. I could dance sylph-like with utter abandon and my partner never got sick to her stomach, even though she had eaten most unwisely."

Or, "At work they were installing a new air-conditioning unit and not once did it fall upon a workman's toes, breaking them permanently."

Or even, "I visited a friend in a hospital, something I once wouldn't have dreamed of doing, and in not one of the rooms that I passed did the intravenous needle pop out of a vein. Nor did a single hypodermic needle miss its appropriate target."

Sometimes, he would ask me, brokenly, "Are you sure that I will have a chance to save humanity?"

"Absolutely," I would say. "That's part of the cure."

But then, one day he came to me and there was a frown on his face. "Listen," he said. "I just went to the bank to ask a question about my bank-balance, which is a little lower than it should be because of the way you manage to get out of restaurants before the bill shows up, and I couldn't get an answer because the computer went down just as I walked in. Everyone was puzzled.—Is the cure wearing off?"

"It can't do that," I said. "Maybe it had nothing to do with you. There might be some other teleklutz around who hasn't been cured. Maybe he happened to walk in just as you did."

But that wasn't it. The bank's computer went down on two other occasions when he tried to check his bank balance. (His nervousness over the paltry sums I had neglected to take care of was quite nauseating in a grown man.) Finally, when the computer at his firm went down when he walked past the room in which it was housed, he came to me in what I can only describe as panic.

"It's back, I tell you. It's back!" he screamed. "I can't

take it this time. Now that I'm accustomed to normality, I can't go back to my old life. I'll have to kill myself.''

''No, no, Menander. That's going too far.''

He seemed to check himself at the edge of another scream and thought over my sensible remark. ''You're right,'' he said. ''That *is* going too far. Suppose I kill you, instead. After all, no one will miss you, and it will make me feel a *little* better.''

I saw his point, but only to a slight extent. I said, ''Before you do anything at all, let me check this out. Be patient, Menander. After all, so far it's only happened with computers, and who cares about computers?''

I left quickly before he could ask me how he was supposed to get his bank balance if computers were always going down at his approach. He was really a monomaniac on the subject.

So was Azazel, on another subject. It seems that this time he was actually involved in whatever he was doing with the two samini, and he was still turning somersaults when he arrived. To this day, I don't know what the somersaults had to do with it.

I don't think he ever actually cooled down, but he did manage to explain to me what happened and then I was faced with having to explain it to Menander.

I insisted on meeting him in the park. I chose a fairly crowded section since I would have to rely on instant rescue if he should lose his head figuratively, and try to make me lose mine literally.

I said, ''Menander, your teleklutzism still works, but only for computers. *Only for computers*. You have my word on that. You are cured for everything else *forever*.''

''Well, then, cure me for computers.''

''As it happens, Menander, that can't be done. You are not cured for computers, and forever.'' I rather whispered the last word but he heard me.

''Why? What kind of a hare-brained, idiotic, malapropistic, oniklutzistic rear end of a diseased Bactrian camel are you?"

"You make it sound as though there are many kinds, Menander, which doesn't make sense. Don't you understand that you wanted to save the world, and that's why it happened?"

"No, I don't understand. Explain it to me and take your time. You have fifteen seconds."

"Be reasonable! Humanity is facing a computer-explosion. Computers are going to become rapidly more versatile, more capable and more intelligent. Human beings are going to be ever-more dependent upon them. Eventually, a computer will be built that will take over the world and leave humanity with nothing to do. It may then well decide to wipe out humanity as unnecessary. Of course, we tell ourselves smugly that we can always 'pull the plug', but you know we won't be able to do that. A computer smart enough to do the work of the world without us will be able to defend its own plug and, for that matter, find its own electricity.

"It will be unbeatable, and humanity will be doomed. And that, my friend, is where you come in. You will be brought into its presence or perhaps you will only arrange to pass within a few miles of it and it will instantly break down, and humanity will be saved! *Humanity will be saved!* Think of it! Think of it!"

Menander thought of it. He didn't look happy. He said, "But meanwhile, I can't come near computers."

"Well, the computer-klutzism had to be nailed down and made absolutely permanent so that we could be sure that when the time came nothing would go wrong; that the computer would not somehow defend itself against you. It's the price you pay for this great gift of salvation that you yourself asked for and for which you will be honored through all future history."

"Yes?" he said, "and when is this salvation to take place?"

I said, "According to Azaz—my sources, it should take

place in sixty years or so. But look at it this way. Now you know that you will live to be at least ninety years old.''

"And meanwhile," said Menander, in a loud voice, oblivious to the way people nearby turned to stare at us, "meanwhile, the world will grow more and more computerized and I will be unable to get near more and more places. I'll be unable to do more and more things and will be in a total prison of my own making—"

"But in the end you will save humanity! That's what you wanted!''

Menander shrieked, "To hell with humanity!" rose and hurled himself at me.

I managed to get away but only because there were people about who seized the poor fellow.

Today, Menander is in deep analysis with a Freudian psychiatrist of the most determined description. It will surely cost him a fortune and will, of course, do him no good whatever.

George, having finished his story, gazed into his pot of beer, for which I knew I would have to pay.

He said, "There's a moral to this story, you know."

"What is it?"

"People just don't have any gratitude!"

NEITHER BRUTE NOR HUMAN

The monthly dinner of the Black Widowers was well under way and Emmanuel Rubin, his fork uplifted, and waving threateningly in the air, temporarily ignored his rack of lamb and said, "Edgar Allan Poe was the first important practitioner of the modern detective story and of the modern science fiction story. I'll give him that."

"Nice of you," murmured James Drake, the host of the occasion, in a low aside.

Rubin ignored him. "He lifted the horror story to new heights, too. Still, he had a morbid and unhealthy preoccupation with death."

"Not at all," said Geoffrey Avalon, in his deep voice, his thick eyebrows lowering into a frown. "Poe was writing in the first half of the nineteenth century, and there was still virtually no protection against infectious disease at the time. Life was short and death was ever-present. He wasn't being morbid; he was being realistic."

Roger Halsted said, "Absolutely! Read any fiction of the nineteenth century. Read Dickens and the death of Little Nell, or Harriet Beecher Stowe and the death of Little Eva. Children frequently died in fiction because they frequently died in real life."

Rubin's eyes, magnified by his thick glasses, took on a stubborn gleam, and his sparse beard seemed to bristle. "It's not death in itself. It's how you treat it. You can deal with it as the doorway to heaven, and treat the dying person as a saint—see the death of Beth in *Little Women*. That can be sickeningly sentimental, but it is meant to be uplifting. Poe, on the other hand, dwells with an unholy glee on the elements of degradation and decay. He makes death worse than it is and—Come on, you all know very well what 'morbid' is."

He returned to his lamb and attacked it with vigor.

Thomas Trumbull growled and said, "Certainly. 'Morbid' is talking about morbidity over what would otherwise be a pleasant dinner."

"I don't see that it makes any difference whether Poe was morbid or not," said Mario Gonzalo, who was neatly dissecting strips of meat off the ribs. "What counts is whether he was a good writer or not, and I suppose no one argues with the fact that he was good."

Avalon said, judiciously, "Even good writers aren't good all the time. James Russell Lowell described Poe as 'three fifths of him genius and two fifths sheer fudge,' and I would say that was pretty accurate."

Halsted said, "My feeling is that a seminal writer has to accept some responsibility for his imitators. There is something about Poe that makes it absolutely necessary for his imitators to be awful. Consider H.P. Lovecraft—"

"No," said Rubin, violently, "we are *not* discussing Lovecraft; we are talking about Poe—"

And oddly enough, Drake's guests, who, until now, had sat mute through the dinner, said suddenly in a loud, almost metallic voice, "*Why* are we talking about Poe?"

His name was Jonathan Dandle; short, plump around the middle, a round face that was now quite flushed, a large bald head with a fringe of white hair about the ears, and round gold-rimmed bifocals. He looked in his early sixties.

He had startled the company into silence, and even Henry, the imperturbable waiter who was the pride of the Black Widowers, allowed an expression of surprise to flit momentarily across his face.

Drake cleared his throat and stubbed out his cigarette. "We talk about anything we please, Jonathan. Poe is as good a subject as any, especially since Manny Rubin writes mysteries so that Poe might be considered his patron saint. Right, Manny?"

Dandle looked about the table from one to the other and some of the redness drained out of his face and left it a normal blue. He lifted his hands in a kind of shrug. "My apologies, gentlemen. It was not my intention to dictate the subject of the conversation."

He looked a trifle unhappy.

Rubin nodded at Dandle in slightly haughty forgiveness, and said, "Actually, if we're talking about the patron saint of mysteries. I could make a good argument in favor of Conan Doyle. The Mystery Writers of America may hand out Edgars, but the archetypical detective, as all of us know—" and, with that, Poe was abandoned.

Dandle listened intently to the further course of the conversation, but said nothing else until Henry had served the coffee, and Gonzalo had produced a quick caricature which he showed the guest.

Dandle regarded it solemnly, then smiled. "It is fortunate, Mr. Gonzalo, that I have no great opinion of my beauty. You make me look like the old-time actor Guy Kibbee. Perhaps you don't remember him."

Gonzalo said, "Certainly, I remember him, and now that you point it out there is a resemblance. A clever artist, with a few strokes of the pen, can bare essentials that are not necessarily obvious."

"What a pity, Mario," said Rubin, "that you don't find a clever artist who can teach you to do so."

"And yet," said Gonzalo easily, "you have met any number of clever writers and none has been able to help you."

At which point, Drake rattled his water glass with his spoon. "Grilling time, gentlemen, so that Manny and Mario are requested to shut up.—Jeff, will you do the honors."

Geoffrey Avalon stirred the melting ice in his half-consumed second Scotch with his middle finger, and said, "Mr. Dandle, how do you justify your existence?"

Dandle said, thoughtfully, "A good question. Since I had nothing to do with the initiation of my existence in this unfortunate world, I might justifiably deny any need to defend myself. However, I have accepted my existence for over six decades now—after all, I might have killed myself easily enough—so I will defend. How would it be if I told you I am making it easier for people to communicate with each other. Would that serve as grounds for justification?"

"It depends on what they communicate," said Gonzalo. "Now Manny's attempts at—"

"Mario!" said Avalon, sharply, and turned a frowning looking in Gonzalo's direction. Then, more gently, he said, "I have the floor and I would rather that we not descend into anarchy this time.—In what way, Mr. Dandle, do you make it easier for people to communicate?"

"I work in fiber optics, Mr. Avalon, and communications by laser light through glass, rather than by electricity through copper, will make for cheaper and thinner cables that would nevertheless carry more messages. I admit that not all the high technology in the world will of itself serve to improve the quality of those messages."

"And yet, sir, if I may be allowed to interject a personal note, you do not yourself show much tendency to communicate, considering that communication is your business.

You have said hardly anything at all during cocktails or dinner. Is there a reason for that?''

Dandle looked about him, his face reddening again. It was quite apparent that he flushed easily, and, like almost all people who do, that he was quite aware of it and seemed the more embarrassed—and to redden more—because of it. He mumbled something.

"I beg your pardon, sir," said Avalon. "I didn't hear you."

Drake, who sat next to his guest, and who looked rather uncomfortable himself, said, "Jonathan, saying, 'I've nothing to say' is no answer."

Dandle said, "It's an answer if that's the answer I choose to give, Jim."

"No," said Drake, peering at his guest out of his wrinkle-nested eyes. "That's not among the permitted choices, Jonathan. I explained the deal on this meeting. You receive a good dinner and good company in exchange for substantive answers. No secrets. No evasions. My own experience is that you've always had plenty to say."

Avalon said, "Let me continue, Jim.—Mr. Dandle, I will accept your answer that you have nothing to say, though I wish you would speak up so that others besides your immediate neighbor might hear you. My next question is this: Why is it that you have nothing to say on this occasion considering that, if we are to believe Jim, such silence is not typical of you?"

Dandle spread out his hands and said loudly enough, "Is a man always accountable for his actions, Mr. Avalon? Does he always know the origins of his moods?"

Avalon said, "Then let me ask you another question. You did, on one occasion, interject a question into the general conversation. You asked why we were talking about Poe, and you did so quite forcibly. I interpreted your remark as indicating that you were offended, perhaps outraged, by the discussion. Is that so? And if it is so, why?"

Dandle shook his head. "No, no. I just asked."

Trumbull stood up and passed one hand over his tightly waved white hair. He said, with exaggerated patience, "Jim, as the host, you must make a decision. We are clearly getting nothing out of our guest, and I think that, under the rules of the club, we might be forced to adjourn the meeting now. In fact, I move you consider adjournment."

Drake waved a hand at him petulantly. "Take it easy, Tom.—Jonathan, you've got to answer honestly. Nothing that is said here will ever be repeated outside these walls. Our waiter, Henry, is a member of the club and he is as closemouthed as we are. More so. I know you well enough to know you haven't committed a crime, or are planning to commit one, but even so, we—"

"You're quite wrong," said Dandle, in a rather more high-pitched voice than before. "I am trying to commit what *I* consider a crime. I'm certainly trying to be dishonest."

Drake said, "You?"

"With what I think is considerable justification, of course."

"After that," said Trumbull, "if Dandle does not care to elaborate, Jim, then we can go no further."

There was silence. Trumbull remained standing. Drake looked at Dandle and said, "Well, Jonathan?"

Dandle said, "You told me, Jim, I would be grilled on the details of my profession. I did not expect this sort of thing."

"It can't be helped. If you had been yourself, none of this would have come up. What's wrong?"

Dandle looked helpless. He clenched his fist, made as though he was going to bring it down on the table, stopped the motion, and said, "It's my sister."

"Your crackp—" began Drake, and stopped suddenly.

"My crackpot sister," said Dandle. "She's dying. Cancer."

There was a sudden silence.

"We've known it for months," said Dandle, "and she

may live for months more, but it does produce problems.''

The silence continued. Finally, Henry said, "Brandy, gentlemen?"

Avalon said, absently, "Just a small portion, Henry.— What kind of problems, Mr. Dandle?"

"Her will."

"You mean, all this is a matter of money?" said Halsted, with rather more than a shade of disapproval in his voice.

"Not money at all," said Dandle, lifting his eyebrows. "Please understand, gentlemen, that my wife and I are well off. We have a son and daughter, but both are grown and both are reasonably well off. My sister has a house and some money that she inherited from our parents, but this is not something we lust for. At least, not the money. That she can dispose of as she wishes. She can leave it to a farm for homeless cats, if she wishes. It's the house."

He fell into momentary thought. "It was quite clear that she would never marry by the time my parents died. It made sense to leave the family house to her, even though it was unnecessarily large for one person. Still, it's belonged to the family since it was built; I was born there; lived there till I married; I have a profound emotional attachment to it. Now my sister, Rachel," Dandle looked briefly at Drake, "being, as you say, a crackpot, is planning to leave it to a crackpot organization, and I don't want her to. I'd be willing to have it sold to someone respectable. I'd even be willing to have it torn down in a decent way for a decent purpose. But I'm damned if I'm willing to let the—the Cosmic Order of Theognostics infest it."

"The *what?*" said Gonzalo.

Avalon said, "The word comes from the Greek and means 'knowing God.' "

Dandle said, "What they really know are methods for extracting money from fools and nuts."

Avalon said, "I assume they are extracting money from your sister."

"To some extent, yes, but not very much. She is a shrewd

woman, financially, and is quite compos mentis outside her obsession. Still, they're angling to get it all when she dies. And they may."

"What is her obsession, sir?"

"I believe it started with her reading of Poe when she was young. I think she read everything he had written; memorized it, just about; and absorbed the unhealthy morbidity that Mr. Rubin mentioned. And she read Lovecraft, too, and grew inclined to believe in horrors from outer space, in elder intelligences, and so on. She lectured me often enough on that stuff. Naturally, she became part of the UFO mania."

"Naturally," muttered Rubin, with a look of distaste.

"She became convinced that intelligent beings from outer space are actually on Earth and have taken over Earth's leaders, and much of the general population. She thinks these aliens are themselves invisible, or can make themselves so, and can live within human beings parasitically. It's all quite mad."

"I suppose," said Avalon, "that if anyone disagrees with her, or tries to argue against her views, she considers it a sign the arguer has been taken over."

"Absolutely. I early on recognized the mistake of trying to oppose her."

Halsted said, "Why haven't the aliens taken over everybody? How does your sister explain that she herself hasn't been taken over?"

"I gather," said Dandle, "that the Cosmic Order of Theognostics fights them with prayer and introspection and meditation and incantation and whatever the devil they claim to do, and they have taught her the same. She has tried to teach me and I've just kept silent and listened. There's a lot of candle burning involved, and the recitation of whole pages of material that has no meaning whatever but I suppose she thinks it keeps me safe—so far."

Drake said, through the smoke of his cigarette, "When I referred to her as a crackpot, Jonathan, I was thinking of the UFO stuff. I didn't know about this alien intelligences bit.''

''It's not something I like to talk about, obviously,'' said Dandle, ''and wouldn't be talking about now except under pressure.''

Avalon said, ''You said you were thinking of committing a crime. Surely, you're not thinking of mayhem against the Theognostics.''

''Nothing like that. Just a crime in my own eyes. I've been trying to cheat and deceive my sister, and I'm not really proud of that.''

''Would you be willing to explain that, sir?'' asked Avalon, stiffly.

''Well, since Rachel was found to have cancer, things are at a crisis. She won't submit to surgery because she is sure that under anesthesia she will be taken over. She is suspicious of radiotherapy, too, since radiation is a weapon of those beings. She is relying entirely on Theognostic ritual, therefore, and you can imagine how effective that is.''

Rubin said, ''The most ridiculous methods can sometimes help if you believe firmly that they will. The mind is a powerful instrument.''

''That may be,'' said Dandle, ''but it isn't helping her. She's going downhill, and, about a month ago, she began to talk of leaving the house and her money to the Theognostics so that they could continue the great fight against the aliens.—So I started a plan of my own.'' He reddened and stopped.

After a short pause, Avalon said, gently, ''Yes, Mr. Dandle?''

''To put it bluntly,'' said Dandle, ''I came to her as an enthusiastic convert. I said she had convinced me and that I was heart and soul with her; that she could leave the money to the Theognostics if she wished, but that she should leave the house to me and I would make it the center of the fight against the aliens. I would allow the Theognostics to use it freely but I merely wanted to keep title to it in honor of our parents. I was hypocritical and obsequious.''

"No doubt," said Avalon, "but did it work? People who, like your sister, believe in invisible, untestable dangers would be suspicious of everything.''

"I'm afraid so," said Dandle. "She's of two minds about me. She *wants* to believe, but, as you say, she is suspicious. She hesitates to tell me what I'm sure she believes to be the 'higher mysteries,' so to speak. I asked for details about the form and attributes of the mysterious aliens, for instance, and she was closemouthed about it—as though she was not sure I was worthy of initiation.''

Trumbull said, "Maybe she doesn't know herself.''

Rubin said, "She can easily invent anything she wishes and then come to believe it. Such things are very common.''

"Last week she said something in a sort of singsong whisper and I thought I was making progress, but then there was nothing more.''

"What did she say?''

"Well, they're hermaphroditic and are neither women nor men. And they weren't Earthly, of course. They aren't human beings or animals. And when they infest us they live on our spiritual nature rather than on our physical bodies, I gather, for she seized my arm, with a surprisingly strong grip, too, and whispered into my ear, 'They are *worse* than cannibals, and that is not surprising considering where they come from.' ''

"Where do they come from?" asked Gonzalo.

"That's what I asked," said Dandle, "but she didn't say. She said that once you achieve a certain enlightenment, you *know* where they come from; that that is the test of enlightenment. It comes over you like a wave of revelation and gives you a certain power against them. *She* knows, and the Theognostics know; but they don't tell anyone because that's their test for the people who are strong against the aliens. It doesn't really make sense, but if I were to try to say that to her, it would mean the end of my chance to save the house. So I just said, earnestly, that I would meditate and try to gain the knowledge.'' He looked about the table with a grim face. ''I'm supposed to be fasting.—She called me this morning.''

''Things are coming to a crisis?'' asked Avalon.

''Yes. That's why I've been preoccupied this evening, and didn't say much. I was of two minds whether to come here at all, but I didn't want to let Jim Drake down.''

''But what was it your sister said to you this morning?''

''She says she wants to make a decision about her will. She feels herself weakening and she knows that she must become one with the Great Divine—which is the Theognostic term for God, apparently—and she wants to make sure she continues the fight from beyond the grave. She can't let me have the house unless she is certain I won't bar the Theognostics from it. And, of course, barring them is *exactly* what I intend to do so I am trying to flimflam her.—It's not exactly admirable of me.''

Trumbull said, loudly, ''We're on your side, Mr. Dandle. You're fighting a group of pernicious and vicious flimflam operators, and if counter-flimflam is required, so be it.''

''Thank you,'' said Dandle, ''but I don't see that I will win out. She wants me to visit her tomorrow at noon and tell her where the aliens come from. If I can't, then she can't rely on me to remain strong against them and the Theognostics will get the house. And, of course, I can't tell her where the aliens come from. They're from outer space, I'm sure. That would fit in with her UFO madness, for they undoubtedly reached Earth by UFO. But where in outer space?''

There was a short silence, then Gonzalo said, ''She never gave you any hints?''

Dandle shook his head. ''Only the remark about their being worse than cannibals and that that somehow was appropriate, considering where they come from. But what does that mean?''

''Nothing else?''

"Not that I can think of. If she did, it went right past me.—So tomorrow I lose the house."

Avalon said, "You know, sir, that you can contest the will."

"No, not really," said Dandle. "You were introduced to me as a lawyer—"

"A patent lawyer," said Avalon. "I am not knowledgeable on the intricacies of testamentary litigation."

"Well, on the one hand, there is a strong tendency to allow a testator to do as he wishes with his own property. It isn't easy to disallow a religious organization in favor of a relative who is already well off. I doubt that I can prove undue influence, nor would I care to try to make my sister seem to have been of unsound mind, if only out of family considerations. Then, even if I really thought I could win, it would be a long-drawn-out fight in which the legal fees would come to considerably more than I would care to pay.—So I'm going to lose the house."

Avalon said, "We might all of us think about this a bit."

A flicker of hope seemed to enliven Dandle. "Are any of you astronomers?"

"Not professionally," said Halsted, "but we have the usual superficial knowledge of the field that any intelligent and reasonably well-read individuals would have."

"Exactly," said Rubin, "and that means I can make a suggestion. We're looking for something in outer space that has cannibalistic associations. I've read articles recently that in clusters of galaxies, there are occasional collisions and that, in such collisions, the larger member gains stars at the expense of the smaller one. The result is that in some clusters, there is one galaxy that is larger than any of the others, having cannibalized them."

Halsted nodded vigorously. "You are right, Manny. I've read about it, too. There's one outsize galaxy that has five small bright regions within itself that resemble galactic centers. The thought is that it swallowed five small galaxies whole."

Gonzalo said, "Just for the record—what are galaxies?"

Avalon said, "Large conglomerations of stars, Mario. Our own Milky Way Galaxy has a couple of hundred billion stars in it."

Gonzalo said, "Well, then, has that cannibal galaxy— the one that swallowed up its five little sisters—got a name?"

The Black Widowers stared at each other. Finally, Halsted said, "It may, but if it does, it's probably not an ordinary name. Just a particular catalog number like NGC– 1111, or something like that."

Gonzalo said, "I don't think Miss Dandle would be impressed by that."

Dandle said, "I don't think so, either. I'm grateful to you for your attempts to help, but if galactic cannibalization is a common phenomenon, which cannibal would be the correct one? And I'm sure my sister knows nothing about modern sophistications in astronomy, anyway. Nor would the Theognostics. Where would they hear of this phenomenon?"

Avalon said, "Does your sister read anything at all in the field of astronomy, Mr. Dandle?"

Dandle said, thoughtfully. "She certainly read everything there is on UFOs and some astronomy—not necessarily correct—is bound to creep in there. She reads up on astrology, of course, which means additional possibly distorted astronomy. And I have seen astronomy popularizations in the house. I haven't actually seen her reading them but I wouldn't be surprised if she did."

"Is she well-read otherwise, sir?"

"Yes. All of Poe as I said, and Lovecraft, and some science fiction. A great deal of general nineteenth-century fiction, I should say, and, of course, she reads the newspapers and a number of magazines thoroughly, if only to find evidence of how far the aliens have taken over the world. I've got to explain to you that there's nothing wrong with her intelligence, outside her—her crackpottery."

"In that case," said Avalon, with a certain sombre satisfaction, "I am quite sure I have the answer." He paused and cast a glance in the direction of the waiter, who was standing at the sideboard, listening with polite but silent attention.

"Henry," said Avalon, "I think that on this occasion we will not need your help."

"Yes, Mr. Avalon," said Henry, quietly.

Avalon cleared his throat. "You see, by far the best-known portion of the Universe, even to astronomers, and *certainly* to the general public, are the planets of our own Solar System. This is especially true for people like Miss Dandle, who are interested in astrology and similar aberrations.

"And of the planets, the one which in recent years has received the most attention and which is, in any case, the most spectacular, is the planet Saturn, with its rings and satellites. The Voyager probes have taken close-up photographs of the Saturnian system and these have made all the newspapers and magazines. Miss Dandle cannot have missed them."

Dandle said, "I'm sure she has not. But what then?"

"Saturn," said Avalon, "is named for an early Roman god of agriculture whom the Romans, with scant justice, equated with the Greek god Kronos. Kronos with his brothers and sisters made up the group of gods called the Titans, and they were the children of Ouranos and Gaea, the god of the sky and the goddess of the Earth, respectively. In a series of most unpleasant myths, the Greeks describe Kronos as castrating his father, Uranus, and taking over the rule of the Universe.

"Since the Fates had decreed that Kronos would, in turn, be replaced as ruler by his own son, the new lord of the Universe took to devouring each child as it was born. His wife, Rhea, managed to save one son by offering Kronos a rock wrapped in the baby's swaddling clothes. The rather stupid Kronos swallowed that without noticing the substitution. The son, still uneaten, was then hidden in Crete, and raised to maturity in secret. Eventually, the son, who was named Zeus (Jupiter, to the Romans), warred upon the Titans, defeated them, released his siblings, who were still alive within Kronos, and took over the Universe. All this Miss Dandle, in her reading, might very well have come across.

"Now, then, Saturn was clearly a cannibal. If there are degrees in such things, devouring one's own children is surely worse than fattening on strangers, so he might well be viewed as worse than an ordinary cannibal. Miss Dandle's statement that the aliens were worse than cannibals and that that was not surprising in view of where they came from would make sense if they came from Saturn."

And Avalon smiled at Dandle with self-conscious triumph.

Dandle said, "You think, then, I had better tell my sister the alien beings come from Saturn?"

"I can't say the matter is certain," said Avalon. "She may, after all, suppose them to have come from some entirely fictitious planet such as Zorkel, the fifth planet of the star Xanadu, in the galaxy of Yaanek. If, however, she has a real astronomical body in mind, then I am virtually certain that it is Saturn. It must be."

"It sounds good to me," said Gonzalo.

"It makes sense," admitted Rubin, looking distressed at having to say so.

Halsted said, "It's worth a try."

Trumbull said, "I can't think of anything better."

Drake said, "It seems unanimous. I'd take the chance, Jonathan."

Dandle began, "Well, since I can't think of anything better, either—"

Gonzalo interrupted. "Wait, Henry hasn't said anything. Henry, what do you think?"

Dandle looked up in astonishment at having the waiter referred to.

When Henry said, "May I ask Mr. Dandle if he shared in his sister's enthusiasm for Poe?" Dandle looked more astonished still.

Drake said, "Please answer, Jonathan. Henry is one of us."

Jonathan said, "No, definitely not. I know 'The Raven'; no one can avoid knowing that; but I know nothing else. I stay away from him."

"In that case," said Henry, "I fear that Mr. Avalon's suggestion, although most ingenious, is not the correct answer."

Avalon looked offended. "Indeed, Henry? Have you anything better to offer?"

Henry said, "Consider, sir, that Miss Dandle was a great devotee of Poe, and that in describing the aliens she said that they were neither female nor male, animal nor human."

"Well?"

"Well, Mr. Avalon, I, unlike Mr. Dandle but like his sister, am an admirer of Poe, though more so of his poetry than of his prose. Among my favorite poems by Poe is 'The Bells,' in the fourth part of which he describes the tolling of the funeral bells. There you have his morbid preoccupation with death, you see, something that is bound to follow his earlier descriptions of sleigh bells, wedding bells, and fire-alarm bells."

"Aha," said Rubin.

"Yes, Mr. Rubin," said Henry, "I suspect you already see what I mean. Part of the description of the funeral bells is—if I may quote:

> "And the people—ah, the people—
> They that dwell up in the steeple,
>   All alone,

And who, tolling, tolling, tolling,
  In that muffled monotone,
  Feel a glory in so rolling
On the human heart a stone—
  They are neither man nor woman—
  They are neither brute nor human—"

Henry paused, then said, "Miss Dandle was undoubtedly quoting those last two lines, I think. You stated that she said them in singsong fashion, Mr. Dandle, but not being a Poe enthusiast, you did not recognize them."

Avalon said, "But even so—How does that help?"

Henry said, "It is the next line that counts, as Poe identifies the people who toll the funeral bells."

And he and Rubin quoted simultaneously: " *'They are Ghouls.'*"

Henry said, "Ghouls are creatures of Middle Eastern legend who infest graveyards and feed on dead bodies. That might well strike Miss Dandle, or anyone, as worse than ordinary cannibalism, just as vultures are worse than hawks in the general estimation."

Avalon said, "I grant that, but I still don't see the point."

"Nor I," said Trumbull.

Henry said, "There is a constellation in the sky named Perseus, named for the Greek hero who cut off the head of Medusa, a creature so dreadful in appearance that anyone looking at it turned to stone. The constellation is pictured as the hero holding the head of Medusa and that head is marked by a second-magnitude star, Beta Persei. I looked it up in the Columbia Encyclopedia during the discussion, to be sure of that fact.

"Because of its position in the constellation, Beta Persei is sometimes called the Demon Star, in consequence. The Arabs, who adopted the Greek view of the sky, named it *Al Ghul*, meaning 'The Ghoul,' their version of something as horrible as Medusa, and our English version of that Arabic name is 'Algol.' That is now the common name of the star.

"Since Miss Dandle quoted that poem to define the aliens, she meant that they were ghouls, and therefore worse than cannibals, and she must have meant that it was not surprising that they were since they came from the star known as 'The Ghoul'—a fact she could surely have picked up from some book on popular astronomy, as I did, originally. I would suggest, then, Mr. Dandle, that you say, when you see your sister tomorrow, that the aliens come from Algol."

Dandle smiled brightly for the first time that evening and broke into applause. "Henry, I will. That *should* be the answer, and I am sure it is."

Henry said, gravely, "Nothing may be completely sure in this case, sir, but it is worth the gamble."

THE FOURTH HOMONYM

"Homonyms!" said Nicholas Brant. He was Thomas Trumbull's guest at the monthly banquet of the Black Widowers. He was rather tall, and had surprisingly prominent bags under his eyes, despite the comparative youthfulness of his appearance otherwise. His face was thin and smooth-shaven, and his brown hair showed, as yet, no signs of gray. "Homonyms," he said.

"What?" said Mario Gonzalo, blankly.

"The words you call 'soundalikes.' The proper name for them is 'homonyms.'"

"That so?" said Gonzalo. "How do you spell it?"

Brant spelled it.

Emmanuel Rubin looked at Brant owlishly through the thick lenses of his glasses. He said, "You'll have to excuse Mario, Mr. Brant. He is a stranger to our language."

Gonzalo brushed some specks of dust from his jacket sleeve and said, "Manny is corroded with envy because I've invented a word-game. He knows the words but he lacks any spark of inventiveness, and that kills him."

117

"Surely Mr. Rubin does not lack inventiveness," said Brant, soothingly. "I've read some of his books."

"I rest my case," said Gonzalo. "Anyway, I'm willing to call my game 'homonyms' instead of 'soundalikes.' The thing is to make up some short situation which can be described by two words that are soundalikes—that are homonyms. I'll give you an example: If the sky is perfectly clear, it is easy to decide to go on a picnic in the open. If it is raining cats and dogs, it is easy to decide *not* to go on a picnic. But what if it is cloudy, and the forecast is for possible showers, but there seem to be patches of blue here and there, so you can't make up your mind about the picnic. What would you call that?"

"A stupid story," said Trumbull, tartly, passing his hand over his crisply-waved white hair.

"Come on," said Gonzalo, "play the game. The answer is two words that sound alike."

There was a general silence and Gonzalo said, "The answer is 'whether weather.' It's the kind of weather where you wonder whether to go on a picnic or not. 'Whether weather', don't you get it?"

James Drake stubbed out his cigarette and said, "We get it. The question is: How do we get rid of it?"

Roger Halsted said, in his soft voice, "Pay no attention, Mario. It's a reasonable parlor game, except that there don't seem to be many combinations you can use."

Geoffrey Avalon looked down austerely from his 72-inch height and said, "More than you might think. Suppose you owned a castrated ram that was frisky on clear days and miserable on rainy days. If it were merely cloudy, however, you might wonder whether that ram would be frisky or miserable. That would be 'whether wether weather'. "

There came a chorus of outraged "What!"'s.

Avalon said, ponderously. "The first word is 'w-h-e-t-h-e-r', meaning ' if.' The last word is 'w-e-a-t-h-e-r', which refers to atmospheric conditions. The middle word is 'w-et-h-e-r', meaning 'a castrated ram.' Look it up if you don't believe me.''

"Don't bother," said Rubin. "He's right."

"I repeat," growled Trumbull. "This is a stupid game."

"It doesn't have to be a game," said Brant. "Lawyers are but too aware of the ambiguities built in to the language, and homonyms can cause trouble."

The gentle voice of Henry, that waiter-for-all-seasons, made itself heard over the hubbub by some alchemy that worked only for him.

"Gentlemen," he said. "I regret the necessity of interrupting a warm discussion, but dinner is being served."

"Here's another one," said Gonzalo, over the smoked trout. "Someone has written down all the digits and on all of them but one he has drawn a very clever face. A child watching this is delighted, but dissatisfied with the incompleteness of the project. What does he say?"

Halsted, who was spreading the horseradish sauce daintily over his trout, said, "The child says, 'Do that to two, too.' "

Gonzalo said in an aggrieved manner, "Have you heard that somewhere before?"

"No," said Halsted, "but it's a mathematical instance of the game. What's the use of teaching mathematics at junior high school, if I can't solve problems involving the number, two."

Gonzalo frowned. "You're trying to be funny, aren't you, Roger?"

"Who me?"

Trumbull said, "As host of the evening, I would like to recommend that we change the subject."

No one gave any sign of hearing. Avalon said, "Homonyms are usually the result of the accidents of language history. For instance, 'night', by which I mean the opposite of 'day', is cognate to the German, 'Nacht,' while 'knight', by which I mean a warrior of the Table Round, is cognate with the German 'knecht'. In English, the vowels changed and the 'k' is invariably silent in an initial 'kn', so you end up with two words pronounced in identical fashion.''

''The initial 'kn' does not invariably have a silent 'k', '' said Rubin. ''There are some words not yet sufficiently Anglicized. I have a Jewish friend, who married a young lady of the Gentile persuasion. Anxious to please her new husband, she bought some ethnic delicacies for him which she displayed proudly. Listing her purchases, she said, finally, 'And I also bought you this nish,' and was quite puzzled when he broke into hysterical laughter.''

Drake said, ''I don't get it.''

Rubin said, with a touch of impatience, ''The word is 'knish'—with the 'k' heavily pronounced. It is a ball of dough in whose interior one places spiced mashed potatoes, or possibly some other filling, with the whole then being fried or baked. Any New Yorker should know that.''

Trumbull sighed and said, ''Well, if you can't lick them, join them. Can anyone give me a group of four homonyms, four words all pronounced alike, with spelling and meaning different in each case? I'll give you five minutes in which I expect blessed silence.''

The five minutes passed pleasantly enough, with only the sound of cracking lobster shells impinging upon the eardrums, and then Trumbull said, ''I'll give you one of the words: 'right' meaning 'the opposite of left.' What are the other three?''

Halsted said, his mouth fairly full of lobster claw, ''There's 'write' meaning 'to inscribe words', and 'rite' meaning 'a fixed religious procedure', but I don't think there's a fourth.''

Avalon said, ''Yes, there is. It's 'wright', 'w-r-i-g-h-t', meaning 'a mechanic.' ''

''That's archaic,'' protested Gonzalo.

''Not entirely,'' said Avalon. ''We still speak of a 'playwright', who would be 'someone who constructs plays.' ''

Brant said, ''My friend, Tom, mentioned 'right', defining it as 'the opposite of left.' What about 'right' meaning 'the opposite of wrong', and 'right' meaning 'perpendicular'? Would that be a fifth and sixth homonym?''

"No," said Gonzalo, "the spelling has to be different for the words to be homonyms.''

Avalon said, "Not always, Mario. Two words can be spelled the same but have different meanings and have different etymological origins; they would count as homonyms. For instance, 'bear' meaning the animal, and 'bear' meaning 'to carry', have the same spelling and pronunciation, but have different origins, so I would call them homonyms; along with 'bare' meaning 'unclothed', of course. The different uses of 'right', however, as in 'right hand', 'right answer', and 'right angle', all stem from the same root with the same meaning, so they would not be homonyms.''

There were fifteen additional minutes before Trumbull felt justified in rattling his spoon against the water glass and bringing the conversation to a halt.

"I have never been so glad," he said, "at any of the banquets of the Black Widowers to put an end to a conversation. If I had absolute power as a host, I would fine Mario five dollars for starting it.''

"You took part in it, Tom," said Gonzalo.

"In self-defense—and shut up," said Trumbull. "I would like to present my guest, Nicholas Brant, and Jeff, you seem civilized even if you were more homonymized than anyone else, so would you do the honors and begin the grilling.''

Avalon's formidable eyebrows lifted, and he said, "I scarcely think that 'homonymized' is English, Tom.'' Then, turning to the guest, he said, "Mr. Brant, how do you justify your existence?''

Brant smiled ruefully. "As a lawyer, I don't think I can. You know the old joke, perhaps, of the time God threatened to sue Satan, and Satan answered, 'How can you? I've got all the lawyers.' In my defense, however, I'm not the kind of lawyer who plays tricks in front of a judge and jury.

Mostly I sit in my office and try to write documents that actually mean what they are supposed to mean.''

Avalon said, ''I'm a patent lawyer myself, so I ask the following question without evil intent. Do you ever try to write them so that they *don't* mean what they're supposed to mean? Do you try to build in loopholes?''

Brant said, ''Naturally, I try to draw up a document that leaves my clients as much freedom of action as possible, and the other side as little freedom of action as possible. However, the other side has a lawyer, too, who is working hard for the reverse, and the usual result is that the contract ends up reasonably iron-bound in both directions.''

Avalon paused, then said, ''In the earlier discussion on homonyms, you said, if I remember correctly, that homonyms are ambiguities that could cause trouble. Does that mean you ran into a homonym professionally, in your preparation of contracts, that brought about unexpected complications?''

Brant raised both hands. ''No, no, nothing like that. What I had in mind when I made that statement was completely irrelevant to the subject now under discussion.''

Avalon ran his finger around the rim of his water glass. ''You must understand, Mr. Brant, that this is not a legal cross-examination. There is no particular subject under discussion, and nothing is irrelevant. I repeat my question.''

Brant remained silent for a moment, then he said, ''It's something that took place a little over twenty years ago, and that I have thought about only very occasionally since then. Mr. Gonzalo's game of homonyms brought it mind, but it's—nothing. It doesn't involve any legal problems or any complications whatever. It's just a—puzzle. It's an insoluble matter that isn't worth discussing.''

''Is it confidential?'' put in Gonzalo. ''Because if it is—''

''Nothing confidential about it,'' said Brant. ''Nothing secret, nothing sensitive—and therefore nothing interesting.''

Gonzalo said, "Anything that's insoluble is interesting. Don't you agree, Henry?"

Henry, who was filling the brandy glasses, said, "I find it so when there is at least room for speculation, Mr. Gonzalo."

Gonzalo began, "Well, then, if—"

Avalon said, "Mario, let me continue, please.—Mr. Brant, I wonder if you could give us the details of this insoluble puzzle of yours. We would greatly appreciate hearing it."

"You'll be very disappointed."

"That's a chance we will take."

"Well, then," said Brant, "if you'll just give me a chance to think back—"

He rested his face in one hand, thinking, while the six Black Widowers watched him expectantly, and Henry took his usual place by the sideboard.

Brant said, "Let me begin with Alfred Hunzinger. He was a poor boy of an immigrant family, and he had no education worth mentioning. I'm pretty sure he never went to high school. By the time he was fourteen, he was working. Those were the decades before World War I and education was by no means considered one's birthright, or even particularly desirable for what used to be called workingmen.

"Hunzinger wasn't your usual workingman, however. He was incredibly industrious and incredibly intelligent. Intelligence and education don't necessarily go hand in hand, you know."

Rubin said, forcefully, "Indeed, they don't. I've known some very thoroughly educated jackasses."

"Hunzinger was the reverse," said Brant. "He was a very thoroughly uneducated business genius. He had a green thumb, but it was the green of dollar bills. Whatever he touched prospered, and he built a formidable business before he died.

"Nor was this enough for him. He always felt keenly his

lack of education, and he embarked on a program of home study. It wasn't continuous, for his business was his first preoccupation and there were periods when he had little time. And it was spotty, for he read promiscuously and without outside guidance. Conversation with him was an exposure to a curious mixture of pedantry and naivete.''

Avalon said, ''You knew him personally, I take it.''

Brant said, ''Not really. Not intimately. I did some work for him. Mainly, I prepared his will. This, when properly done, and when there are complex business matters to consider, takes a long time and produces a long document. Periodically, it must be updated or revised, and the wording considered carefully in the light of continually changing tax laws. Believe me, it was virtually a career in itself and I was forced to spend many hours in conference with him and to engage in extensive correspondence, too. However, it was a very limited and specialized relationship. I got to know the nature of his finances rather thoroughly, but to know him, as a person, only superficially.''

''Did he have children?'' asked Halsted.

''Yes, he did,'' said Brant. ''He married late in life; at the age of 42, if I remember correctly. His wife was considerably younger. The marriage, while not idyllically happy, was a successful one. There was no divorce nor any prospect of one at any time, and Mrs. Hunzinger died only about five years ago. They had four children, three boys and a girl. The girl married well; she's still alive, still married, has children of her own, and is, and has been, very comfortably off. She scarcely figured in the will. Some investments were turned over to her during Hunzinger's lifetime and that was it.

''The business was left on an equal basis, one-third each, to the three sons, whose names were Frank, Mark and Luke.''

''In that order of age?'' asked Drake.

''Yes. The oldest was, to use his legal signature, B. Franklin Hunzinger. The middle son is Mark David Hunzinger. The youngest son is Luke Lynn Hunzinger. Naturally, I pointed out to Hunzinger that to leave his business in equal shares to his three sons was asking for trouble. The income might be divided equally, but the directing power, the decision-making power, had to be placed in the hands of one.

"He was very stubbornly resistant to that, however. He said he had brought up his sons in accordance with the ideals of the old Roman republic; that they were all faithful to him, the paterfamilias—he actually used the term, to my intense surprise—and to each other. There would be no trouble at all, he said.

"I took the liberty of pointing out that they might well be ideal sons while he was alive and with his forceful personality directing affairs. After he was gone, however, hidden rivalries might show up. Never, he insisted, never. I thought him blind, and wondered how anyone so alive to any hint of chicanery in business affairs, so realistic in matters of the world, could be so foolishly romantic where his own family was concerned."

Drake said, "What was the daughter's name?"

"Claudia Jane," said Brant. "I don't remember her married name at the moment. Why do you ask?"

"Just curious. She might have had ambitions, too, mightn't she?"

"I don't think so. At least not with respect to the business. She made it quite clear she neither expected nor wanted any share in it. Her husband was rich—old money—social position—that sort of thing. The last thing she wanted was to be identified with what was—in a manner of speaking—a giant hardware store."

"Well, I see that," said Drake.

"I must admit that the family seemed entirely harmonious," said Brant. "I met the sons at one time or another, singly and together, and they seemed fine young men, much at ease with one another, and obviously fond of their father. What with one thing and another, I reached the stage where it seemed appropriate to invite me to the festivities celebrating the old man's eightieth birthday. It was on that occasion that Hunzinger had the heart attack that carried him off. It was not entirely unexpected. He'd had a heart condition for years, but it was totally unfortunate for it to happen on his birthday.

"The party broke up, of course. He was laid, gently, on the nearest couch and doctors were called in. There was a kind of hushed pandemonium. The confusion was sufficient for me to be able to stay on. It may sound ghoulish, but I conceived myself to have a job to do. He had not yet assigned any son to be the head of the firm. It was too late to have anything in writing; but if he would say something, it might have some force.

"The sons, I suppose, did not know what I had in mind. They were there, of course. Their mother, half in shock, had been led away. No one seemed to notice I was present. I leaned across to the old man's ear and said, 'Which of your sons is to be the head of the firm, Mr. Hunzinger?'

"It was too late. His eyes were closed, his breathing was stertorous. I wondered if he had heard me. A doctor approached and I knew he would stop me, so I tried again quickly. This time, the dying man's eyelids fluttered, and his lips moved as though he were trying to speak. However, only one sound came out. It seemed to be the word 'to'. I heard nothing else. He lingered on for another hour but never said another word, and died, without regaining consciousness, on the couch on which he had been laid.—And that's it."

Gonzalo said, "What happened to the business?"

"Nothing," said Brant, with what seemed the residuum of a vast surprise. "The old man was right. The three sons get along famously. It's a sort of triumvirate. When a decision must be made, they get together and come to one quickly. It's really an amazing thing and if that sort of thing should become infectious, lawyers would all starve to death."

"Then it doesn't matter what the old man said, does it?" said Gonzalo.

"Not in the least, except that for a while it roused my curiosity. What was he trying to say? You see the difficulty, I suppose?"

"Of course," said Drake, fingering his small gray mustache. "You can't do much with the word 'to.'"

"It's worse than that," said Brant. "Which homonym? Was it t-o, or t-o-o, or t-w-o. There are *three* to's in the English language. Incidentally, how so you write that sentence? I've often wondered. You can *say* 'three to's', since all three are pronounced alike, but how do you write it, since each one of the homonyms is spelled differently?"

Avalon said, "I would say, 'There are three words pronounced t-o-o.' The double-o is the most unambiguous way of indicating the pronunciation that all three share and you spell it out."

"Well, in any case, even if I knew which t-o-o it was, it wouldn't help me."

Trumbull said, "Mightn't it not have been a word, Al? Suppose he were saying a longer word such as 'constitution.' That's four syllables and he managed to sound only the third. All you'd have would be t-o-o."

"Maybe," said Brant. "I can't prove that that's not so. Just the same, at the time, I got the impression that it was a word, one of the three t-o-o's, however you want to spell it. I suppose I was desperately trying to read his lips and he might have said 'Headship to so-and-so' and all I got was the 'to'. Which leaves me with nothing. Of course, as I said, it doesn't matter. The sons are doing well. Still—"

Brant shook his head. "I'm a lawyer. It bothers me that I came so close to having it done *right*. Even if he were refusing to choose anyone. Even if he were saying 'Not to anyone', he would have been expressing his last wish and that would have been better than just falling into a situation by default. So for a while I kept wondering, and now you've put it back in my head, and I'll keep on wondering for another while.——And getting nowhere because there's no-where to be gotten.''

A heavy silence descended about the table, one which was finally broken by Gonzalo who said, ''At least it's an interesting version of the game of homonyms. Which of the soundalikes was it?''

Trumbull said, ''What's the difference? Not one of the three would help us make sense of what the old man was trying to say.''

''I told you,'' said Brant, glumly. ''It's an insoluble problem. There just isn't enough information.''

''We don't have to *solve* it,'' said Halsted, ''since there's no crisis that has to be eased, or criminal on whom we must visit retribution. All we have to do is point out a reasonable possibility to ease your mind. For instance, suppose he was saying t-w-o.''

''Well, suppose he was,'' said Avalon.

''Then it may be that he was saying something like, 'Give it to son number two.' ''

Brant shook his head, and said, ''The impression I got was that the t-o I heard was in the middle of the message. His lips moved before and after I heard the t-o.' ''

Rubin said, ''I'm not sure you can go by that. His lips were scarcely under control. Some of what appeared to be movement might have been only trembling.''

''Which makes it all the worse,'' said Brant.

''Now wait a while,'' said Halsted. ''My idea works even with the word in the middle of the message. It could have been something like 'Give it to number two son', or 'Number two son gets it.' ''

Trumbull growled, ''Charlie Chan might say it, but was Hunzinger likely to do so.——Al, did you ever hear this man refer to his children by number.''

''No,'' said Brant. ''I don't think I ever did.''

''Well, then,'' said Trumbull, ''Why on earth should he start doing so on his deathbed?''

''I wonder,'' said Rubin. ''Consider this. His second son

is named Mark, which is also the name of the writer of the second gospel. His third son is named Luke, which is the name the writer of the third gospel. I'll bet that if he had had a fourth son, that son's name would have been John.''

"What's the good of a bet like that?" said Gonzalo. "We can't ever settle it and decide on a winner."

"Why wasn't the first son's name Matthew, then?" asked Avalon.

Rubin said, "Maybe old Hunzinger didn't think of it till after the first son was born. Maybe he simply didn't like 'Matthew'. Anyway, it strikes me that if the word *were* 'two', it would have a double meaning. It would refer to the second son and the second gospel and it would mean Mark in either case."

Trumbull said, "There could be a million reasons why the number, two, might point to Mark, but put them all together and they wouldn't be any more likely to get him to refer to 'my number two son' than just one reason would. Why wouldn't he just say 'Mark', if he meant Mark?"

Brant said, "Well he might have said 'to Mark' at that and all I heard was 'to.'"

Avalon said, "Mr. Brant, I wonder if you at any time noted that old Mr. Hunzinger trusted one of his sons more than another, valued more highly the business acumen of a particular son, loved one more."

Brant bent his head in thought. Then he shook it. "I can't say I did. I have no recollection of anything of the sort. Of course, as I said, my relationship with the family was not a matter of warm personal friendship. It was business, entirely. The old man never confided family matters beyond anything that was relevant to the will."

Gonzalo said, "We keep talking about the sons. How do you know the old man didn't give some thought to his daughter? Suppose he left the business to his three sons, in thirds, but wanted his daughter to make crucial decisions. He might have thought she had the best business sense and should run the show even though she wouldn't want to be connected with the business in any open way.''

"What gives you that idea, Mario?" asked Avalon.

"Suppose the word was t-o-o. He might have been saying, 'My daughter, too, should be involved.' Something like that."

"I don't think so," said Brant. "Mr. Hunzinger never mentioned his daughter in connection with the business. Remember, too, that his prejudices are pre-World War I, when women couldn't even vote. In no way was he a feminist. His wife was strictly a homebody and that's the way he liked it. He took care to have his daughter marry a rich man, and as far as he was concerned, that was the limit of his responsibility toward her. At least, I am forced to that conclusion as I think of our various discussions of the will."

Again, there fell a silence around the table, and finally Avalon said, with a rather theatrical sigh, "It doesn't matter what hypotheses we set forward. No matter how clever and ingenious they might be, there's no way in which we can show that they are true. I'm afraid that this once we have to decide that our guest is correct and that the problem, by its very nature, is insoluble."

Gonzalo said, "Not until we ask Henry."

"Henry?" said Brant, in surprise. His voice dropped to a whisper. "Do you mean the waiter?"

Trumbull said, "No need to whisper, Al. He's a member of the club."

"So I'll ask him," said Gonzalo. "Henry, do you have any ideas about this?"

From his place at the sideboard, Henry smiled very slightly and said, "I must admit, Mr. Gonzalo, that I've been wondering what the first name of the eldest son might be."

Gonzalo said, "Frank. Don't you remember?"

"I beg your pardon, Mr. Gonzalo, but I seem to recall the oldest son is B. Franklin Hunzinger. I wondered what the B stood for."

All eyes turned to Brant, who shrugged and said, "He's

identified as B. Franklin even in his father's will. That's the legal form of his signature. I always assumed, however, that the B stood for Benjamin.''

"It's a natural assumption," said Henry. "Any American named B. Franklin, it would seem, would be bound to be a Benjamin. But did you ever hear any member of the family, or anyone for that matter, address him as Benjamin or Ben.''

Slowly, Brant shook his head. "I don't recall any such incident, but it was over twenty years ago and I was not really part of the family circle.''

"Or since the death of the elder Hunzinger?''

"Oh, well, I've rarely had any contact with them at all since then, not even with respect to legal matters.''

Trumbull said, "What's all this about, Henry?''

"Why, it occurred to me that there are, in a manner of speaking, four homonyms with the sound t-o-o.''

Avalon said, in an astonished voice, "Four? You mean that one of the homonyms has two meanings of unrelated derivation as in the case of b-e-a-r?''

"No, Mr. Avalon. I am referring to four homonyms with four different spellings.''

Avalon thought briefly, "Impossible, Henry. Manny, can you think of a fourth homonym beyond t-o, t-o-o, and t-w-o.''

"No," said Rubin, flatly, "there is no fourth homonym.''

Henry said, "I said 'in a manner of speaking.' It all depends on the first name of B. Franklin.''

Drake said, "Henry, you're being mysterious and you've got us all confused. Now *explain*.''

"Yes, Dr. Drake. Mr. Brant had said that the elder Hunzinger was self-educated, and he had indicated that he was particularly interested in Roman history. He raised his children in what he thought was the Roman tradition. He used terms such as 'paterfamilias' and so on. And he gave his children traditional Roman names. His daughter he named

Claudia; one son is Mark, from the Roman Marcus; another is Luke from the Roman Lucius.

"It is possible, in fact, that the original names were indeed Marcus and Lucius, and that the youngsters found Mark and Luke more palatable to their peers. Now what if the eldest had a Roman name also, which had no common Anglicized form. He might not have used it at all, but stayed with Franklin, which becomes the very common and acceptable Frank.

"One common Roman name beginning with B is Brutus, and that has no Anglicized form that is likely to be acceptable."

"Aha," said Rubin.

"Yes, Mr. Rubin," said Henry. "If the elder Mr. Hunzinger had picked up scraps of Latin, undoubtedly Julius Caesar's last words, one of the most famous of all Latin phrases, would be known to him. It contains the word 'tu' which is Latin for the familiar form of 'you,' and is so well known among educated English-speaking people—if only from this phrase—that it might almost rank as a fourth homonym.

"Asked about which of his sons should head the firm, the dying man thought of the oldest, remembered the name he had been given him as a child and may have said something like 'all my sons share, and you, Brutus, will lead.' The phrase 'and you, Brutus' becomes the muttered Caesarian exclamation of 'et tu, Brute', and only the 'tu' was loud enough to hear."

"Good God," muttered Brant, "who could possibly think of something like that?"

"But it's *most* ingenious," said Avalon. "I hope you're right, Henry. I'd hate to see that reasoning wasted. I suppose we could call Hunzinger and try to persuade him to give us his first name."

Gonzalo said, excitedly, "Wait, Jeff, wouldn't it be in *Who's Who in America*? They usually include businessmen."

Avalon said, "They might well have only the legal version of his name—B. Franklin Hunzinger. Of course, they sometimes include the name beyond the period in parentheses to indicate it exists but is not to be used."

"Let's see," said Gonzalo. He took down the first volume of the tome and for a few moments there was the sound of flipping pages. Then it stopped and Gonzalo cried out in triumph, "Brutus Franklin Hunzinger, the r-u-t-u-s in parentheses."

Brant buried his head in his hands. "Twenty years, on and off, this had bothered me, and if I had looked him up in *Who's Who*—But why would it occur to me to look him up." He shook his head. "I must tell them. They will have to know."

Henry said, "I don't think that would be wise, Mr. Brant. They get along well as it is, but if they find out that their father had chosen one of them to head the firm—which even as it is we can't be *certain* of—bad feelings might break out. Surely one shouldn't attempt to fix what isn't broken."

THE EYE OF THE BEHOLDER

George and I were sitting on a bench at the boardwalk and contemplating the broad expanse of the beach and the sparkling sea in the distance. I was immersed in the innocent pleasure of watching the young ladies in their bikinis and wondering what they could get out of the beauties of life that was half as much as they contributed.

Knowing George as I did, I rather suspected his own thoughts to be considerably less nobly esthetic than mine. I was certain that they would deal with the more useful aspects of those same young ladies.

It was with considerable surprise, then, that I heard him say, "Old man, here we sit, drinking in the beauties of nature in the shape of the female form divine—to coin a phrase—and yet surely true beauty is not, and cannot be, so evident. True beauty, after all, is so precious that it must be hidden from the eyes of trivial observers? Have you ever thought that?"

"No," I said, "I've never thought that and, now that

you mention it, I still don't. What's more, I don't think that you have ever thought that.''

George sighed. ''Talking with you, old chap, is like swimming in molasses—very little return for very great effort. I have watched you observing that tall goddess there, the one whose wisps of fine textile do nothing to conceal the few square inches they purport to cover. Surely, you understand that those are mere superficialities that she displays.''

''I have never asked for much out of life,'' I said, in my humble way. ''I'll be satisfied with superficialities of that sort.''

''Think how much more beautiful a young woman would be—even a woman quite unprepossessing to the untutored eyes of one such as you—if she possessed the eternal glories of goodness, unselfishness, cheerfulness, uncomplaining industry, and concern for others; all the virtues, in short, that shed gold and grace on a woman.''

''What I'm thinking, George,'' I said, ''is that you must be drunk. What on earth can you possibly know about virtues such as those?''

''I am totally familiar with them,'' said George, haughtily, ''because I practice them assiduously, and to the full.''

''Undoubtedly,'' I said, ''only in the privacy of your own room and in the dark.''

Disregarding your crude remark [George said] I must explain that even if I did not have personal knowledge of these virtues, I would have learned of them through my acquaintance with a young woman named Melisande Ott, nee Melisande Renn, and known to her loving husband, Octavius Ott, as Maggie. She was known to me as Maggie also, for she was the daughter of a dear friend of mine, now, alas, deceased, and she always considered me her Uncle George.

I must admit that there is a bit of me, that like you, appreciates the subtle qualities of what you call 'superficialities.'—Yes, old boy, I know I used the term first but we will not get anywhere if you are going to interrupt me constantly over trivialities.

Because of this small weakness in myself, I must also admit that when, in an excess of joy at seeing me, she would squeal and throw her arms about me, my delight at the event was not quite as great as it would have been had she been more generously-proportioned. She was quite thin and her bones were painfully prominent. Her nose was large, her chin weak, her hair rather lank and straight and pure mouse in color, and her eyes an undefinable gray-green. Her cheekbones were broad so that she rather resembled a chipmunk that had just completed a fine collection of nuts and seeds. In short, she was not the type of young woman whose arrival on the scene would cause any young man present to begin breathing rapidly and striving to get closer.

But she had a good heart. She bore up, with a wistful smile, at the visible winces that shook the average young man who met her for the first time, without warning. She served as bridesmaid for all her friends in turn with a fresh group of wistful smiles. She served as godmother to innumerable children, and as baby-sitter to others, and was as deft a bottle-feeder as you could see in a long month of Sundays.

She brought hot soup to the deserving poor, and to the undeserving as well, though there were some who said that it was the undeserving who more nearly deserved the visitation. She performed various duties at the local church, several times over—once for herself and once each for those of her friends who preferred the guilty splendors of the movie palaces to selfless service. She taught classes at Sunday school, keeping the children cheerful by making (as they thought) funny faces at them. She also frequently led them all in a reading of the nine commandments. (She left out the one about adultery for experience had taught her that this invariably led to inconvenient questions.) She also served as a volunteer at the local branch of the public library.

Naturally, she lost all hope of getting married somewhere

about the age of four. Even the chance of having a casual date with a member of the opposite sex seemed to her to be a rather impossible dream by the time she had reached the age of ten.

Many a time she would say to me, "I am not unhappy, Uncle George. The world of men is sealed to me, yes, always excepting your dear self and the memory of poor pappa, but there is far more true happiness in doing good."

She would then visit the prisoners in the county jail in order to plead for repentance, and for conversion to good works. It was only one or two of the crasser sort who volunteered for solitary confinement on those days on which she was due to arrive.

But then she met Octavius Ott, a newcomer to the neighborhood, a young electrical engineer with a responsible position at the power company. He was a worthy young man—grave, industrious, persevering, courageous, honest and reverent—but he was not what you or I would call handsome. In fact, not to put too fine a point on it, he was not what anyone in recorded history would have called handsome.

He had a receding hairline—or, more accurately, a receded one—a bulbous forehead, a snub nose, thin lips, ears that stood well away from his head, and a prominent Adam's apple that was never entirely still. What there was of his hair was rather rust-colored, and he had an irregular sprinkling of freckles on his face and arms.

I happened to be with Maggie when she and Octavius met in the street for the first time. Both were equally unprepared and both started like a pair of skittish horses suddenly confronted by a dozen clowns in a dozen fright wigs who were blowing a dozen whistles. For a moment, I expected both Maggie and Octavius to rear and whinny.

The moment passed, however, and each successfully weathered the flash of panic they had experienced. She did nothing more than place her hand on her heart as though to keep it from leaping out of the rib cage in search of a more secure hiding place, while he wiped his brow as though to erase a horrid memory.

I had met Octavius some days before and so I was able to introduce them to each other. Each held out a tentative hand as though not anxious to add the sense of touch to that of vision.

Later that afternoon, Maggie broke a long silence and said to me, "What an odd young man that Mr. Ott seems to be."

I said, with that originality of metaphor which my friends all enjoy, "You mustn't judge a book by its cover, my dear."

"But the cover exists, Uncle George," she said, earnestly, "and we must take that into account. I dare say that the average young woman, frivolous and unfeeling, would have little to do with Mr. Ott. It would be a deed of kindness, therefore, to show him that not all young women are totally heedless, but that one at least does not turn against a young man for nothing more than his unfortunate resemblance to— to—" She paused as no comparable member of the animal kingdom occurred to her, so that she had to end lamely, but warmly, with "whatever it is that he resembles. I must be kind to him."

I do not know whether Octavius had a confidant to whom he could unburden himself in similar fashion. Probably not, for few of us—if any—are blessed with Uncle Georges. Nevertheless, I'm quite certain, judging from later events, that precisely the same thoughts occurred to him—in reverse, of course.

In any case, each labored to be kind to the other, tentatively and hesitantly at first, then warmly, and at last passionately. What began as casual encounters at the library, became visits to the zoo, then an evening at the movies and at dances, until, finally, what took place could only be described—if you'll excuse my language—as trysts.

People began to expect to see one whenever they saw the

other, for they had become an indissoluble pair. Some of those in the neighborhood complained bitterly that to get a double dose of Octavius and Maggie was more than the human eye could be expected to endure, and more than one supercilious elitist invested in sunglasses.

I will not say that I was totally lacking in sympathy for these extreme views, but others—more tolerant and, perhaps, more reasonable—pointed out that the features on one were, by some peculiar chance, quite opposite to the corresponding features of the other. Seeing the two together tended to introduce a cancelling effect, so that both together were more endurable than either separately. Or at least, that was what some claimed.

Finally, there came a day when Maggie burst in on me and said, "Uncle George, Octavius is the light and life of my existence. He is staunch, strong, steady, sturdy and stable. He is a lovely man."

"Internally, my dear," I said, "I'm sure he is all of these things. His outward appearance, however, is—"

"Adorable," she said staunchly, strongly, steadily, sturdily, and stably. "Uncle George, he feels about me as I feel about him, and we are going to be married."

"You and Ott?" I said, faintly. An involuntary image of the likely issue of such a marriage swam before my eyes and I turned rather faint.

"Yes," she said. "He has told me that I am the sun of his delight and the moon of his joy. Then he added that I was all the stars of his happiness. He is a very poetic man."

"So it seems," I said, dubiously. "When are you going to be married?"

"As soon as possible," she said.

There was nothing to do but grit my teeth. The announcement was made, the preparations were carried through, the marriage was performed with myself giving away the bride. Everyone in the neighborhood attended out of disbelief. Even the minister allowed a reverent look of astonishment to cross his face.

Nor did anyone seem to gaze gladly at the young couple. All through the ceremony, the audience stared at its various knees. Except the minister. He kept his eyes firmly fixed on the rose window over the front door.

I left the neighborhood some time after, took up lodgings in another part of the city and rather lost touch with Maggie. Eleven years later, however, I had occasion to return over a matter of an investment in a friend's learned studies of the racing qualities of horses. I seized the opportunity of visiting Maggie, who was, among her other well-hidden beauties, a marvelous cook.

I arrived at lunch time. Octavius was away at work, but that didn't matter. I am not a selfish man and I gladly ate his portion in addition to mine.

I could not help but notice, however, that there was a shade of grief on Maggie's face. I said, over the coffee, "Are you unhappy, Maggie? Is your marriage not going well?"

"Oh, no Uncle George," she said, vehemently, "our marriage was made in heaven. Although we remain child-less, we are so wrapped up in each other that we are barely aware of the loss. We live in a sea of perpetual bliss and have nothing more to ask of the universe."

"I see," I said, my teeth rather on edge, "then why this shade of grief I seem to detect in you?"

She hesitated, and then burst out, "Oh, Uncle George, you are such a sensitive man. There *is* one thing that does interpose a bit of grit in the wheels of delight."

"And that is?"

"My appearance."

"Your appearance? What is wrong—" I swallowed and found myself unable to finish the sentence.

"I am not beautiful," said Maggie, with the air of one imparting a well-hidden secret.

"Ah!" I said.

"And I wish I were—for Octavius' sake. I want to be lovely just for him."

"Does he complain about your appearance?" I asked cautiously.

"Octavius? Certainly not. He bears his suffering in noble silence."

"Then how do you know he is suffering?"

"My woman's heart tells me so."

"But, Maggie, Octavius is himself—well—not beautiful."

"How can you say that?" said Maggie, indignantly. "He's gorgeous."

"But perhaps he thinks *you're* gorgeous."

"Oh, no," said Maggie, "how could he think that?"

"Well, is he interested in other women?"

"Uncle George!" said Maggie, shocked. "What a base thought. I'm surprised at you. Octavius has no eyes for anyone but me."

"Then what does it matter if you are beautiful or not?"

"It's for *him*," she said. "Oh, Uncle George, I want to be beautiful for *him*."

And, leaping into my lap in a most unexpected and unpleasant way, she moistened the lapel of my jacket with her tears. In fact, it was wringing wet before she was quite through.

I had by then, of course, met Azazel, the two-centimeter extraterrestrial I may have mentioned to you on occa—Now, old man, there is no need for you to mutter 'ad nauseam' in that supercilious manner. Anyone who writes as you do should be embarrassed at bringing up the thought of nausea in any connection whatever.

In any case, I called up Azazel.

Azazel was asleep when he arrived. He had a bag of some green material covering his tiny head and only the muffled sound of quick soprano squeaking from within gave evidence that he was alive. That, and the fact that every once in a while his little sinewy tail stiffened and vibrated with a tinny hum.

I waited several minutes for him to wake up naturally, and when that did not happen, I gently removed his head-bag with a pair of tweezers. His eyes opened slowly and focussed on me, whereupon he gave an exaggerated start.

He said, "For a moment I thought I was merely having a nightmare. I didn't count on *you!*"

I ignored his childish petulance and said, "I have a task for you to do for me."

"Naturally," said Azazel sourly. "You don't suppose I am expecting you to offer to do a task for me."

"I would, in a moment," I said, suavely, "if my inferior abilities were sufficient to do anything a personage of your stature and power would find of significant use."

"True, true," said Azazel, mollified.

It is truly disgusting, I might add, at the susceptibility of some minds to flattery. I've seen you, for instance, go out of your mind with fatuous joy when someone asks you for an autograph.—But back to my tale—

"What is involved?" asked Azazel.

"I wish you to make a young woman beautiful."

Azazel shuddered. "I'm not sure I could bring myself to do that. The standards of beauty among your bloated and miserable species of life are atrocious."

"But they are ours. I will tell you what to do."

"You will tell *me* what to do," he shrieked, vibrating with outrage. "You will tell *me* how to stimulate and modify hair follicles, how to strengthen muscles, how to grow or dissolve bone? Indeed? You will tell *me* all this."

"Not at all," I said, humbly. "The details of the mechanism that such a deed would require are only to be handled by a being of your magnificent attainments. Allow me, however, to tell you the superficial effects to be achieved."

Azazel was once again mollified, and we went over the matter in detail.

"Remember," I said. "The effects are to be brought to

fruition over a period of at least sixty days. A too-sudden change might excite remark."

"Do you mean," said Azazel, "I'm to spend sixty of your days supervising and adjusting and correcting? Is my time worth nothing in your opinion?"

"Ah, but you could then write this up for one of your world's biological journals. It is not a task that many on your world would have the ability or patience to undertake. You will be greatly admired as a result."

Azazel nodded, thoughtfully. "I scorn cheap adulation, of course," he said, "but I suppose I have a duty to hold myself up as a role model for inferior members of my species." He sighed with a shrill, whistling sound. "It is troublesome and embarrassing, but it is my duty."

I had a duty as well. I felt I ought to remain in the neighborhood during the interval of change. My horse-racing friend put me up in return for my expertise and advice on the results of various experimental runnings, with the result that he lost very little money.

Each day I sought an excuse to see Maggie and the results slowly began to show. Her hair grew fuller-bodied, and developed a graceful wave. Red-gold glints began to appear, lending it a welcome richness.

Little by little, her jawbone grew more prominent, her cheekbones more delicate and higher. Her eyes developed a definite blue that deepened from day to day to what was almost violet. The eyelids developed just the tiniest oriental slant. Her ears grew more shapely and lobes appeared. Her figure rounded and grew almost opulent, bit by bit, and her waist narrowed.

People were puzzled. I heard them myself. "Maggie," they would say. "What have you done to yourself? Your hair looks simply marvelous. You look ten years younger."

"I haven't done *anything*," Maggie would say. She was as puzzled as all the others were. Except me, of course.

She said to me, "Do you notice any change in me, Uncle George?"

I said, "You look delightful, but you have always looked delightful to me, Maggie."

"Maybe so," she said, "but I have never looked delightful to me until recently. I don't understand it. Yesterday, a bold young man turned to look at me. They always used to hurry by, shading their eyes. This one *winked* at me, however. It caught me so by surprise, I actually smiled at him."

A few weeks later, I met her husband, Octavius, at a restaurant, where I was studying the menu in the window. Since he was about to enter it to order a meal, it was the work of a moment for him to invite me to join him and the work of half another moment for me to accept.

"You look unhappy, Octavius," I said.

"I *am* unhappy," he said. "I don't know what's got into Maggie lately. She seems so distracted that she doesn't notice me half the time. She wants to be constantly socializing. And yesterday—" A look of such woebegone misery suffused his face that almost anyone would have been ashamed of laughing at it.

"Yesterday?" I said. "What of yesterday?"

"Yesterday she asked me to call her—Melisande. I can't call Maggie a ridiculous name like Melisande."

"Why not? It's her baptismal name."

"But she's my Maggie. Melisande is some stranger."

"Well, she has changed a bit," I said. "Haven't you noticed that she looks more beautiful these days?"

"Yes," said Octavius, biting off the word.

"Isn't that a good thing?"

"No," he said, more sharply still. "I want my plain, funny-looking Maggie. This new Melisande is always fixing her hair, and putting on different shades of eye-shadow, and trying on new clothes and bigger bras, and hardly ever talking to me."

The lunch ended in a dejected silence on his part.

I thought I had better see Maggie and have a good talk with her.

"Maggie," I said.

"Please call me Melisande," she said.

"Melisande," I said. "It seems to me that Octavius is unhappy."

"Well, so am I," she said, tartly. "Octavius is getting to be such a bore. He won't go out. He won't have fun. He objects to my clothes, my makeup. Who on earth does he think he is?"

"You used to think he was a king among men."

"The more fool, I. He's just an ugly little fellow I'm embarrassed to be seen with."

"You wanted to be beautiful just for him."

"What do you mean *wanted* to be beautiful. I *am* beautiful. I was always beautiful. It was just a matter of developing a good hair-style and knowing how to fix my makeup just right. I can't let Octavius stand in my way."

And she didn't. Half a year later, she and Octavius were divorced and in another half-year Maggie—or Melisande—was married again to a man of superficial good looks and unworthy character. I once dined with him and he hesitated so long at picking up the check, I was afraid I might have to pick it up myself.

I saw Octavius about a year after his divorce. He, of course, had not re-married, for he was as odd-looking as ever and milk still curdled in his presence. We were sitting in his apartment which was filled with photos of Maggie, the old Maggie, each one more atrocious than the next.

"You must still be missing her, Octavius," I said.

"Dreadfully!" he replied. "I can only hope she is happy."

"I understand she isn't," I said. "She may come back to you."

Sadly, he shook his head. "Maggie can never come back to me. A woman named Melisande may wish to come back

but I couldn't accept her if she did. She isn't Maggie—my
lovely Maggie.''

"Melisande,'' I said, "is more beautiful than Maggie.''

He stared at me for a long time. "In whose eyes,'' he
said. "Certainly, not in mine.''

It was the last time I saw either.

I sat for a moment in silence, then I said, "You amaze
me, George. I was actually touched.''

It was a poor choice of words. George said, "That re-
minds me, old fellow—Could I touch you for five dollars
for about a week. Ten days tops.''

I reached for a five-dollar bill, hesitated, then said,
"Here! The story is worth it. It's a gift. It's yours.'' (Why
not? All loans to George are gifts *de facto*.)

George took the bill without comment and put it in his
well-worn wallet. (It must have been well-worn when he
bought it, for he never uses it.) He said, "To get back to
the subject. Could I touch you for five dollars for about a
week. Ten days tops.''

I said, "But you *have* five dollars.''

"That is *my* money,'' said George, "and no business of
yours. Do I comment on the state of your finances when
you borrow money from me?''

"But I have never—'' I began, then sighed and handed
over five dollars more.

THE QUIET PLACE

Emmanuel Rubin, who was host of the Black Widowers banquet that evening, had been at his loudest and most quarrelsome.

He had insisted on the unimportance of algebra to Roger Halsted who taught the subject in a junior high school; denounced the patent system to Geoffrey Avalon, who was a patent lawyer; denied the validity of quantum theory in connection with molecular structure to James Drake, the chemist; pointed out the uselessness of espionage in modern warfare to Thomas Trumbull, the cipher expert; and finally placed the cherry on the sundae by watching Mario Gonzalo, as, with consummate ease and skill, he drew a cartoon of that evening's guest, and telling him he knew nothing at all about caricature.

Trumbull, who, of all the Black Widowers, was least likely to be amused by Rubin in his wilder moments, finally said, "What the devil is wrong with you, Manny? We're used to having you wrong at the top of your voice, and taking on one or another of us with some indefensible point of view, but this time you're tackling us all.''

It was Rubin's guest who answered Trumbull in a quiet voice and, at that, it was almost the first time he had spoken that evening. He was a young man, not far gone into his thirties, it would appear, with thin blond hair, light blue eyes, a face that was wide across the cheekbones, and a smile that seemed to come easily and yet had something sad about it. His name was Theodore Jarvik.

''I'm afraid, gentlemen, the fault is mine, if it be a fault to follow professional procedure. I have recently become Manny's editor and I was forced to hand back his latest manuscript with requests for revision.''

''For eviscerative revision,'' muttered Rubin.

''I did offer to cancel out the invitation for this evening,'' said Jarvik, with his sad smile, ''on the supposition that Manny would just as soon not look at me right now.''

Gonzalo raised his eyebrows and said, ''Manny doesn't mind this sort of thing. We've all heard him say about a thousand times that the true professional writer takes revisions and even rejections in stride. He says that one way you can tell an amateur or a beginner is by noting that he considers his every word sac—''

''Oh, shut up, Mario,'' said Rubin, clearly chafing. ''You don't know the details.''

''Actually,'' said Jarvik, ''Manny and I will work it out.''

Avalon, from his 74 inches of height said, in his grave baritone, ''I'm curious, Manny, have you called Mr. Jarvik a 'young punk' yet?''

''Oh, for God's sake,'' said Rubin, reddening.

''No, he hasn't, Mr. Avalon,'' said Jarvik, ''but he's *thought* it very loudly.''

''That is not true,'' shouted Rubin, at the top of his considerable decibel rating.

''Let's wash out this night,'' said Drake, in resignation. ''You're going to be in such a foul humor, Manny, that—''

''When have I *ever* been in a foul—'' began Rubin and

then, Henry, the pearl-beyond-price of waiters, interrupted.

"Gentlemen, please be seated," he said. "Dinner is served."

To due Rubin justice, he did his best to control himself during the dinner. His eyes, behind his thick glasses, flashed; his sparse beard bristled; and he snarled unceasingly; but he managed to say little and leave the conversation to the others.

Gonzalo, who sat next to Jarvik, said to him, "Pardon me, but you keep humming."

Jarvik flushed again, something his fair skin made easy. "I'm sorry, I didn't mean to disturb you."

"It doesn't exactly disturb me. It's just that I don't recognize the tune."

"I don't know. I'm just improving, I suppose."

"Is that so?" and Gonzalo was quiet for the remainder of the dinner until the rattle of spoon on glass marked the beginning of the questioning of the guest.

Gonzalo said, "May I volunteer to do the grilling?"

"You can for all of me," growled Rubin, who, as host, had the task of appointing the griller. "Just don't ask him to justify his existence. The editor doesn't live who can do that."

"On the contrary," said Gonzalo, "any editor who has handed back a manuscript of yours has already justified his existence a hundred times over."

Halsted said, "May I suggest we go ahead with grilling out guest and not needling each other?"

Gonzalo brushed some imaginary dust off the sleeve of his loudly checked jacket and said, "Exactly. Mr. Jarvik, during the course of the dinner I asked you what tune you were humming and you said you were improvising. I don't think that's quite right. Once or twice you hummed again after that and it was always the same tune. Now that you are being grilled, you are forced to give full and honest answers, as I hope Manny has explained to you. I therefore repeat: What was the tune you were humming?''

Trumbull intervened. ''What kind of stupid question is that?''

Gonzalo turned a haughty face on Trumbull. ''As the griller, I am under the impression I can ask any question I choose consistent with human dignity. Host's decision.''

''Go ahead, Manny,'' said Rubin, thus appealed to. ''Ask away.—And leave him alone, Tom.''

Gonzalo said, ''Answer the question, Mr. Jarvik.'' And when Jarvik still hesitated, Gonzalo said, ''I'll help you out. This is the tune,'' and he hummed a few bars.

Avalon said, at once, ''I know what that is. It's 'The Lost Chord.' The music is by Arthur Sullivan of the Gilbert and Sullivan operettas. Except for those operettas, Sullivan is known only for the music to two songs. One is 'Onward, Christian Soldiers' and the other is the aforementioned, 'The Lost Chord.' ''

''Is that what you were humming, Jarvik?''

''I suppose so. You know how a song gets trapped in your mind and won't get out.''

There was a chorus of agreement from the others and Avalon said, sententiously, ''It's a universal complaint.''

''Well, whenever I'm trapped in some sort of loudness,'' said Jarvik, ''that song keeps going through my head.''

Drake chuckled. ''If you're going to be dealing with Manny, you'll be humming it till either you or he dies.''

Gonzalo said, ''Does it have some significance in that connection? What are the words?''

''I only know a few words, actually.''

''*I* know the words,'' said Avalon.

''Don't sing them,'' cried out Trumbull in sudden alarm.

Avalon, whose singing voice was well-known to resemble the sound of an alligator in heat, said, with dignity, ''I shall recite them. The words are by a lady named Adelaide Anne Proctor, concerning whom I know nothing, and the poem goes as follows:'' (He cleared his throat)

"Seated one day at the organ, I was weary and ill at
   ease
And my fingers wandered idly over the noisy keys.
I don't know what I was playing, or what I was
   dreaming then;
But I struck one chord of music, like the sound of a
   great Amen.
It flooded the crimson twilight, like the close of an
   angel's psalm,
And it lay on my fevered spirit with a touch of infinite
   calm.
It quieted pain and sorrow, like love overcoming strife;
It seemed like the harmonious echo from our
   discordant life.
It linked all perplexed meanings into one perfect peace,
And trembled away into silence as if it were loth to
   cease.
I have sought, but I seek it vainly, that one lost chord
   divine,
Which came from the soul of the organ, and entered
   into mine.
It may be that Death's bright angel will speak in that
   chord again,
It may be that only in Heaven shall I hear that grand
   Amen."

There was a short silence and then Halsted said, "You
know, I wonder about that. I don't know how many different
chords you can strike on a large organ considering all the
different stops you can push and pull and the things you do
with your feet. I suppose it is a very large number indeed
and you're not likely to find a particular chord just by fooling
around at random."

Rubin said, testily, "We'll leave it to your mathematical
bent to work out the total number of chords, Roger. As for
you, Ted Jarvik, we can at least see why you hum that song
when things are noisy. All that talk about infinite calm and

one perfect peace and trembling away into silence. Naturally, your mind reverts to the song.''

"No," said Jarvik quietly, shaking his head, "that's not it.''

"Hah," shouted Gonzalo in triumph. "I knew it. I knew it. I have a sixth sense about these things. What is it? What does that song mean to you?''

"Quiet, Mario," said Avalon. "Now, Mr. Jarvik, if Mario has managed to touch a sore point, something about which you do not like to speak, please do so anyway. I assure you nothing you say will ever leave this room.''

Jarvik looked about at the assembled Black Widowers in bewilderment, and said, "How did this ever manage to come up? It's a sore point, certainly, but I can talk about it without trouble. It's just something that's totally uninteresting to anyone but me.''

"You can never tell," said Gonzalo, grinning.

Henry refilled the brandy glasses, and Jarvik sighed and began:

I'm a quiet man said Jarvik as perhaps you can tell. I'm told it shows. There's something ironic in the fact that I have to live and work in Manhattan, but a man must earn a living.

Still, I'm a single man; I don't have a wife and children to support—not yet, anyway—and I can indulge myself now and then. So, two or three times a year I take a week off and go to a resort up the Hudson river. It's a large rambling mansion, with a Victorian atmosphere. The clientele is composed largely of people who are middle aged or older and everything about the place is staid and respectable. Even the young people who happen to come there, are impressed, or perhaps *oppressed*, by the atmosphere and behave themselves.

It means that it is quiet to some degree and, at night, particularly, it is very quiet. Soothing. I love it and, naturally, I try to escape even the noise that exists. People will talk after all and since there are hundreds in the house at all times, the talk can mount up. There are also vehicles—trucks, lawn-mowers and so on.

However, the place is set in an estate of thousands of acres of hilly woodland laced by road and pathways, some of which are very rough indeed. It's my particular pleasure to walk those pathways, looking for some place where I can see only trees and huge glacier-brought rocks, seat myself in one of the gazebos that dot the roads and look at the wildness of the scenery and listen to the silence. There are, of course, the calling of the birds, the rustling of the leaves—but that is no bother. Such natural sounds simply punctuate and emphasize the silence.

But no matter where I go, where I sit, sooner or later, usually sooner, I can hear human voices. There are groups, tramping on nearby trails, or following along the one I just took. I always found it irritating and would feel invaded. It's silly, I know. After all, I was only one of hundreds, but I felt I ought to be undisturbed. I would get up and keep on wandering, looking always for a quiet place, a really quiet place—and never finding it.

One time, as I was sitting in one of my favorite gazebos, a man passed, looked at me, hesitated a moment, and said, in half a whisper, "May I join you?"

I nodded. I couldn't refuse, though I resented him at once; and I couldn't rise and immediately leave without being unbearably discourteous.

After we had been there, in utter silence, some five minutes, the inevitable sound of conversation came from up the road, and there was an explosion of feminine laughter. My new-found companion grimaced and said, "Isn't that annoying?"

My heart warmed to him at once. I shook my head. "You can't get away from it."

He said, "In one place you can," then stopped short as though he had been trapped into saying too much. But I waited with an inquiring look on my face, and didn't say anything, and he said, "There's a place I discovered three-four years ago.—Would you like to see it?"

"Quiet?"

"Oh, yes."

"That would be nice."

"Come with me." He rose, and looked about as if he were taking his bearings. It was a beautifully sunny day, clear blue sky, unclouded, not too warm at all, so when he set off, I followed gladly.

I didn't like to speak, but finally, I had to say, "I haven't seen you about."

"I'm usually out on the trails."

"So am I," I said, my heart warming further. "Ted Jarvik is my name," I said, putting out my hand.

He took it and shook it heartily. "Call me Dark Horse," he said.

And at this point, he suddenly walked right into the woods and began scrambling through and around the underbrush. I was glad I had on a pair of slacks. Had it been warmer, I might have been in shorts and I would undoubtedly have been plant-scratched and insect-bitten. As it was, I followed dutifully.

I couldn't make out where he was going. There was no path and we were clambering over boulders as though we were mountain-climbing. Despite the coolness of the day, I was puffing, hot, and sweaty before long. Finally, we stopped for a bit under the hemlocks and my companion said, "I usually stop here to catch my breath. It takes me longer these days."

I panted a bit, welcoming the break, and said, "How do you know where you're going?"

"Landmarks. A tree that looks just so. A rock with a particular pattern of moss. I notice these things automatically and don't forget them. It's just a knack, but I never get lost."

I said, ruefully, "You're lucky. I have no sense of direction at all. I get irretrievably lost in hotel corridors. Maids have to take me by the hand and lead me to my room.''

My companion laughed and said, ''I'm sure you have many talents. My inability to get lost is the only one I've got.''

''You said your name is Dark Horse. You're not an Indian, are you? A Native American?'' I was staring at him. He looked as little an Indian as I did.

''Not at all. It's not my name. I just said to call me that. You see I believe if you really want to come out on a vacation, you should shuck all the paraphernalia of your ordinary life. I have to give my real name to the hotel, because I have to make a reservation and I have to use my credit card, but while I'm here, I won't be called by my name. Nor will I talk about my business. I simply won't recognize any part of my ordinary self. Whatever I am, officially, is back in Manhattan. It isn't here.''

I was struck by that. ''Interesting idea. I ought to do the same. Not that I'm very social when I come up here.''

He said, ''Rested a bit? Let's go then. We don't have much farther.''

I tried to watch where he turned and to observe landmarks, but it was no use. I'm not a noticing man. To me, a tree is a tree and a rock is a rock.—But then we half-slid downward into a hollow and Dark Horse whispered, ''This is it.''

I looked about. The rocks enclosed us on almost every side. There were trees growing between them here and there. Ferns flourished. It was cool, very cool, welcomingly cool.

Above all else, it was quiet. There was not a sound. A rustle of leaves now and then. A faint insect stridulation. Once a brief bird call. But it was quiet, a healing silence in a world which was one large, long, eternal cacophony of noise.

There was a rocky ledge at a convenient height and my companion indicated it silently. We sat down and I let the silence flow into me. What did the poem say? 'It lay on my fevered spirit with a touch of infinite calm.'

We sat there half an hour and in all that time, I said nothing, and my companion said nothing, and there was not a human sound of any kind. No distant laughter, no crackle of far-off conversation, no vibration of any internal-combustion engine. Nothing. I had never experienced anything like it.

Finally, my companion rose and without saying anything asked the question as to whether we ought to go now. Reluctantly, and without saying anything, I answered that we might.

Out we went. We were a quarter mile away before I dared speak. "How did you find the quiet place?" I asked.

"Accident at first. Since then, I've gone back half a dozen times at least. I love it. It's somewhere out of reach of all the trails and, as far as I know, it's not on any of the hotel maps and it's just a hidden undiscovered nook, known only to me, I think—and now you."

"Thanks for showing me. Really," I said, with infinite gratitude. "You wouldn't think there would be a spot untrodden by human feet in a place like this."

"Why not?" said Dark Horse. "I imagine that all over the world, there are little areas undisturbed by humanity, sometimes in places that are very busy and crowded overall. There are fewer than there used to be, I'm sure, and perhaps someday they'll be all gone—but not yet, not yet."

He led me back to one of the main trails without hesitation. We scrambled over rocks and roots and through the underbrush again and to me it seemed it was uphill both ways—but he got us back. I said good-bye and thanked him again and we shook hands. I went back to the room, got cleaned up and was eventually ready for dinner.

I didn't see him at dinner, though I looked and, in fact, I didn't see him again during the remainder of the stay. To put it baldly, I have never seen him again from that day to this.

The day after he had taken me to the quiet place, I tried to return on my own. I took a book with me and some

sandwiches I had begged at the kitchen, and it was my
intention to stay there most of the day if the weather held,
but of course I never made it. I had no luck at all. I was
wrong from the first turning, I believe.

I didn't give up, though. After I returned to the city, I
kept dreaming of the quiet place and as soon as I could
manage, I returned to the resort, studied the map and marked
off the area that I felt must contain it. I could make my
way to the gazebo where I met Dark Horse and, from there,
I set about a systematic course of exploration.

It did me no good whatever. I could never find the place.
No matter how I tried to remember the twists and turns; no
matter how I kidded myself into believing I recognized one
of those blasted trees or rocks, no matter what bogs I slogged
through, what crags I stumbled over, I ended up nowhere.
I had bites, and scratches, and bruises, and contusions, and
sprains. What I didn't have was the place.

I think it's become an obsession with me. I happened to
know that passage of "The Lost Chord" and I suppose I
began to hear it go through my head with appropriate
changes in words, "I have sought, but I seek it vainly, That
one lost place divine, From which came the spirit of silence
that entered into me."

And I suppose I hum it when things grow loud and cha-
otic—

There was a pronounced pause when Jarvik concluded.

Finally, Halsted said, "I suppose you simply need this
fellow who took you there to take you there again so that
you can mark off each twist and turn on the map as best
you can."

Gonzalo said, hesitantly, "I suppose the fellow really
existed. You didn't dream it, did you?"

Jarvik frowned. "Believe me, I didn't dream it. And he
wasn't an elf leading me into fairyland, either. It happened
exactly as I told you. The problem is that he had a precise
sense of direction and I have none at all."

"Then you ought to find him," said Rubin, flatly, "if you're that stuck on being in the middle of nowhere."

"Fine," said Jarvik. "I agree. I ought to find him. Now tell me how. I don't know his room number. I don't know his name. It didn't occur to me to try to identify him at the front desk that evening or the next day."

He shook his head and seemed to debate with himself whether to go on or not. Then he shrugged and said, "I might as well tell you how obsessed I've become. The last time I was at the resort, I spent half the day with the various desk-employees trying to get a list of the people who had been at the hotel the day on which I was taken to the quiet place.

"It took a lot of negotiating and a lot of scurrying through records, and then they were kind enough to make me up an alphabetized list containing two hundred forty-nine names. They did it for me because I was a regular customer and because I spread fifty dollars among them.

"They didn't include addresses because they said that was against policy and if they were caught doing that they would be fired and blacklisted and who knows what else. I had to make do with the list of names. I made one last effort to find the place the next day—and failed, of course, and then spent the remainder of the stay studying the list of names.

"And you know, I've memorized them. Not on purpose, of course. I just memorized them. I can rattle them off in the alphabetical order in which they were arranged. I happen to have one of those memories." He brooded a little, "If my sense of direction were as good as my memory for trivial items on a list; that is, if my sense of observation could give me small variations I could then remember; I suppose I wouldn't be in the fix I am now."

Drake said, frowning through the smoke of his cigarette, "How would the list of names help you?"

Jarvik said, "The first thing that occurred to me was that the false name he used must have some reason behind it.

Why would anyone call himself Dark Horse? Possibly because the initials were the same as those of his real name. So I went through the list and there was only one D. H. and the name was Dora Harboard. Well, whatever my friend was, he was not a woman, so that was out.

"Then I thought that perhaps the initials were reversed. So I looked for an H. D. and there was none. Then I looked for unattached males. A great many people were listed as, let us say, Ira and Hortense Abel, to take the first names on the list. It seemed to me I ought to eliminate them, especially if they had children with them. That left me with seventeen unattached males and at first I thought that that was a big advancement.

"But then I realized that Dark Horse gave me no indication that he was unattached. He might well have had a wife and child back in his room, or out attending the mah jong game that was being played in the lounge that afternoon."

Trumbull said, "You could try *force majeure*. Follow up every male name on the list and see if one of them is Dark Horse. Who knows, you may strike it lucky the first name you try. And you know he lives in Manhattan. He said so. Try the phone book to begin with."

Jarvik said, "One of the people listed is S. Smith. I dread the thought of how many Smiths there are in the phone book with S as the first initial. Besides, if I recall correctly, he said that whatever he was officially was back in Manhattan. It seems to me that meant he worked in Manhattan but not necessarily that he lived there. He could live in any of the five boroughs, or in New Jersey, or Connecticut, or Westchester.

"Listen, I've thought of *force majeure*. Just to show you, I thought that I might hire someone at some small nearby airfield to fly me over the resort so that I could see the spot from above, but I know I wouldn't recognize it. Not from above, in a hurried pass. And even if I did, they'd have to land me back at the airport and if I then tried to reach the quiet place from the ground I'd fail again.

"Then I thought that perhaps I could hire a helicopter and if I recognized the spot, I could have myself lowered by some sort of rope while the helicopter hovered overhead. That's ridiculous, though. I wouldn't have the nerve to dangle from a helicopter even if I recognized the place and then, after I left it, what if I still couldn't find my way back. I couldn't very well use a helicopter every time, could I?"

Gonzalo said, "Dark Horse! Isn't that a racing term?"

"Originally, yes," said Avalon. "It refers to some horse of unknown potential that might have an outside chance to win, especially if it enters a race in which all the other horses are known quantities."

"Why *dark* horse, then?" said Halsted.

"I presume," said Avalon, "as an indication of how minimal the information is. After all, most horses are dark in coloring. Besides, 'dark' gives the impression of mystery, of the unknown."

"Well," said Gonzalo, "perhaps this fellow has some connection with the racing game."

Jarvik said, bitterly, "Fine. Suppose he does. How does that help me find him?"

"Besides," said Trumbull. "It seems to me that 'dark horse' has spread out to mean anyone who enters a contest without being a known item. In boxing, tennis; in politics, even."

"And how does *that* help me find him?" said Jarvik.

Avalon sighed heavily and said, "Mr. Jarvik, why don't we look at 'The Lost Chord' from another angle? Roger Halsted pointed out that a complex organ might have many, many varieties of chords and that one chord could be easily lost among the quantity. But that is surely a way of looking at it that is rather too simplistic.

"Any sensation consists of the sensation itself, objectively, and of the person receiving the sensation, subjectively. The same chord is always the same chord if it is measured by an instrument that analyzes its wave function. However, the chord one *hears* may well vary with the mood and immediate circumstances of the listener.

"The person playing the organ in the poem was 'weary and ill at ease.' For that reason, the chord had a particular effect on him. 'It quieted pain and sorrow' which he may have been feeling. From then on, when he sought the chord again, his mood would be one of anxious expectation, of careful attention. Even if he heard the same chord again, the *same* chord precisely, it would not strike him in the same way and he would not consider it to be the same chord. No wonder he sought it vainly. He was seeking to duplicate not only the chord but himself as he had been."

Jarvik said, "You are saying?"

"I am saying, Mr. Jarvik," said Avalon, "that perhaps you ought to attach less importance to the place. You found it on a perfect day. You found it when someone else was guiding you there so that you were, in a sense, carefree. If you find it again a second time, it may be on a less desirable day—when it is hotter, or colder, or cloudier. You yourself will be seeking anxiously, you will not be at ease. The result is that it may not be the same place you remember. You will be bitterly disappointed. Would it not be better to remain with the memory and let it go at that?"

Jarvik's head bent and for a few moments, he seemed lost in thought. Then he said, "Thank you, Mr. Avalon. I think you're right. If I fail to find the place, I will certainly try to follow your advice and find solace in it. However— I would like, if I can, to find it once more, just to make sure. After all, Dark Horse found it a number of times, and enjoyed it each time."

"Dark Horse knew how to get there," said Avalon. "His own mood was fairly constant, and it might be he always chose days of particularly favorable weather to go there."

"Even so," said Jarvik, stubbornly. "I would like to find it once more, if there were only a way of finding it."

"But apparently there isn't," said Avalon. "You must admit that."

"I don't know," said Mario. "No one has asked Henry."

"In this case," said Avalon, stubbornly, "even Henry can do nothing. There is nothing to seize on."

"What have we to lose?" demanded Mario. "Henry, what can you tell us?"

Jarvik, who had been listening in astonishment, now turned to Rubin and jerking his thumb over his shoulder, mouthed silently: The waiter?

Rubin put a finger to his lips and shook his head slightly.

Henry, who had been listening with absorption, said, "I must say that I agree fully with Mr. Avalon with respect to the subjective nature of the charms of the place and would hate to have Mr. Jarvik spoil an idyllic memory. Nevertheless—"

"Aha," said Gonzalo. "Go on, Henry."

Henry smiled in his avuncular fashion, and said, "Nevertheless, the one thing to seize upon is the phrase 'dark horse', which everyone has been seizing upon, as it happens. May I ask, Mr. Jarvik, if, by any chance, there was anyone on the list named Polk—not a very common name. A James Polk, perhaps."

Jarvik's eyes opened wide. "You're kidding."

"Not at all. May I take it there *was* such a name?"

"There's a J. Polk certainly. It could be James."

"Then perhaps that is your man."

"But why?"

"Mr. Trumbull mentioned I believe that 'dark horse' is used in politics. That, I suspect, is its most common use these days. A dark horse is some politician who is never thought of in connection with nomination by a major party, but who is nevertheless nominated as a way of breaking what otherwise seems an intransigeant deadlock. Nowadays, dark horses rarely show up because the nomination is decided by primary contests. However, as recently as 1940,

Wendell Willkie was a dark horse named by the Republican party.

"However, the name is most often used in American history for the very first party nominee who was a dark horse. In 1844, the Democrats were all set to nominate ex-President Martin Van Buren, but he needed a two-thirds majority and intransigeant Southern opposition prevented that. Out of sheer weariness, the convention switched to Tennessee Senator, James Knox Polk, whom no one had thought of in connection with the nomination. He was the first dark-horse candidate, and went on to win the election. He made a pretty good one-term President."

"He's right," said Rubin. "Do you know everything, Henry?"

"No, Mr. Rubin," said Henry, "but I had a dim memory of it and while the discussion was going on, I checked our reference shelf. It may be that the J. Polk on Mr. Jarvik's list is a lineal, or collateral descendant, which is why he took the name of Dark Horse."

"Amazing," muttered Jarvik.

"However," said Henry, "you may still have trouble finding him, Mr. Jarvik, and even if you find him, he may still be the wrong person, and even if he is the right person, you may still end up disappointed in the quiet place. However—may good luck be with you."

I LOVE LITTLE PUSSY

George and I were sitting on a park bench on a perfect late spring day when a rather ordinary tabby cat wandered into our vicinity. I knew there were feral cats in the park that would be dangerous to approach, but this specimen had the inquisitive look of a tame pussy. Since I am proud of the fact that cats are attracted to me, I held out my hand and sure enough she sniffed at it and allowed me to stroke her head.

I was rather surprised to hear George mutter, "Wretched little beast."

"Don't you like cats, George?" I asked.

"Would you expect me to, in the light of my sad history?" he said, sighing heavily.

"I know your history is sad," I said. "Inevitably so, considering your character, but I didn't know that cats had a role in it."

"That," said George, "is because I never told you of my second cousin, Andromache."

"Andromache?"

167

• • •

Her father [said George] was a classical scholar, hence the name. He also had a little money, which he left to Cousin Andromache on the occasion of his early death and she, by shrewd investment, considerably increased it.

He did not include me in his bounty. I was a child of five at the time of his death and he could scarcely have left me anything outright, but a more generous soul would have set up a trust fund.

As I grew older, however, I realized that Cousin Andromache, who was 22 years older than I, might well predecease me. It did occur to me—for I was a precocious lad, thoughtful and far-sighted—that, in that case, I might receive a sizable share of the loot.

—Yes, provided, as you say, that I sucked up to her. Please do not try to anticipate my words, however, for that is not the phraseology I intended to use. What I was going to say was that I realized I might inherit a portion of her estate if I gave her the warmth and affection she so richly deserved.

As it happened, Cousin Andromache needed warmth and affection not only richly, but also desperately. When I was still in my teens and she was approaching forty, I realized that she was a dedicated spinster, untouched by human hands. Even at my tender age, I found the situation understandable. She was tall and rawboned, with a long plain face, large teeth, small eyes, limp hair, and no figure worth mentioning.

I said to her once, out of a natural curiosity to determine how unlikely an event might be and yet come to pass, "Cousin Andromache, has any fellow ever asked you to marry him?"

She turned a threatening face on me and said, "Asked me to marry *him*? Hah! I'd like to see some fellow ask me to marry *him*!"

(I rather thought she would indeed like to see it happen,

but I had early reached the years of discretion and did not put the thought into words.)

She went on, "If any man ever has the *gall* to ask me to marry *him*, I'll give *him* what for. I'll show *him* a thing or two. I'll teach *him* to approach a respectable woman with any of his lollygagging notions."

I didn't quite see what was lollygagging about a marriage proposal, or what might be in it to offend a respectable woman, but I didn't think it would be wise—or even safe—to ask.

For a few years, I kept hoping that some person, perverse enough to be interested in Cousin Andromache, might indeed make a suggestion or two because I wanted to see what she would do—while I remained at a safe distance, to be sure. There seemed, however, no chance of that. Not even her gathering wealth seemed to suffice to make her an object of marriageability to the male half of the population. One and all, it seemed, weighed the price that would have to be paid, and one and all turned away.

An abstract consideration of the situation showed me that it was exactly what I wanted. A Cousin Andromache without husband and without children would be less apt to dismiss a second cousin as a testamentary possibility. Furthermore, since she was an only child, the vicissitudes of life had left her with no relative closer than I was. That seemed an appropriate situation for me, since it meant I didn't have to work too hard at supplying affection. A little bit, now and then, to reinforce my position as the natural heir, would be quite enough.

When she passed that fortieth milestone, however, it must have seemed to her that if no human male wished to dare her wrath with a proposal of marriage, she would make use of a non-human companion, instead.

She disliked dogs, because she had the notion that, one and all, they lusted to bite her. I would have liked to reassure her that no dog, however gaunt, would find her a toothsome morsel, but I had the feeling this would not reassure her, and would cripple me, so I kept silent on the matter.

She also thought that horses were too large for comfort, and hamsters too small, so she finally persuaded herself that what she wanted was a cat.

Thereupon, she obtained a little grey female kitten of nondescript appearance and bestowed every bit of her ungainly affection upon it.

With an appalling lack of even a modicum of wit, she named the kitten "Pussy" and that name was retained by the cat forever after, despite changes in size and temperament.

What's more, she took to cuddling the kitten and saying, in a revoltingly hoarse sing-song:

"I love little pussy, her coat is so warm
And if I don't tease her, she'll do me no harm.
I'll pet her and stroke her, and give her some food,
And pussy will love me because I'm so good."

It was simply nauseating.

I won't conceal from you, old man, that I was quite perturbed at first. Thoughts danced through my mind of besotted old maids who left all their money to their pampered, uncaring pets.

It did occur to me, as to whom would it not, that the kitten could easily be kidnapped and drowned, or taken to the zoo and fed to the lions, but then Cousin Andromache would merely get another.

Besides, she might suspect me of a hand in the felicide. Considering the paranoia peculiar to spinsters, I knew that it was perfectly possible for her to get it into her head that I was primarily after her money and that she could interpret many things in that light and come fearsomely near the truth. In fact, I strongly suspected that she had already gotten it into her head.

It occurred to me, therefore, to invert matters. Why not display a passionate love of the kitten? I took to playing moronic games with it, dangling a piece of string for it to fight with, stroking it (sometimes, a little longingly, in the region of its neck), and feeding it tid-bits—sometimes even (when Cousin Andromache was watching) from my own plate.

I must say it worked. Cousin Andromache softened distinctly. I presume she reasoned that I couldn't possibly be after Pussy's money, for she had none, so she chalked it up to the pure and unalloyed love I had for all of God's creatures. I helped strengthen that notion by telling her, in fervent tones, of how pure my love for them was. It made her accept my love for her with fewer fears concerning any ulterior motives I happened to have.

However, the trouble with a kitten's that eventually it becomes a cat.—Oh, did Ogden Nash say that also? Well, my best bits are constantly being stolen. I'm quite resigned to it.

I don't know, old man, if you have ever owned a cat, but with age, they grow larger, more self-centered, more self-assured, more contemptuous of their owners, more inert, more utterly uninterested in anything but food and sleep. The last thing on their contemptible little minds is the comfort and peace of mind of the person who feeds them.

In addition, Pussy grew rather ill-tempered. It had always seemed to me that tabby cats are comparatively placid and that it is the tomcats who are aggressive. It was clear, however, that Pussy had the disposition of a tomcat, despite her sex,—and an unaltered tomcat at that. What's more, she seemed quite intolerant of me and would deliberately go out of her path in order to pass near me and scratch me surreptitiously. I tell you, old man, I could almost believe the beast could read my mind.

Considering Pussy's disposition, it is not at all surprising that Cousin Andromache went into a small decline. I found her in tears one day, or as close to tears as her tough and scraggy temperament would allow her to be.

"Oh, Cousin George," she said to me, "Pussy doesn't love me."

Pussy was, at the time, sprawled in comfort five feet away and was looking at Cousin Andromache with haughty distaste—its usual expression except when it looked at me, at which time the expression became one of settled hate.

I called the creature to my side, whereupon it favored me with a sneer and a bit of a snarl and stayed where it was. I strode to her and picked her up. She weighed 14 pounds of solid inertia and the task was not an easy one, particularly since she kept adjusting her right forepaw (the most dangerous one) into a position where a rapid swipe could be made.

I clutched both her forepaws to prevent that, whereupon she hung in such a way as to double the pull of gravity upon her. I believe that only cats and truly obnoxious human infants know the secret and I am constantly surprised that scientists do not investigate the phenomenon.

I placed her in Cousin Andromache's lap, pointed at the tableau and said, "See, Cousin Andromache, Pussy loves you."

But I had taken my mind off the malignant devil, so that she had the chance of biting my pointing finger, and promptly did so to the bone. She then got off Cousin Andromache's lap and walked away.

Cousin Andromache wailed, "You see, she doesn't love me!" Characteristically, she said nothing about my massacred finger.

I sucked bitterly at the damage and said, "That's the way cats are. Why not give Pussy to someone you hate and get a new kitten."

"Oh, no," said Cousin Andromache, turning on me one of her censorious looks. "I love little Pussy. Isn't there some way of training a cat to display affection?"

I longed to make some clever comment to the effect that it would be easier to train Cousin Andromache to be pretty, and was able to suppress the longing only because a brilliant idea had illuminated the interior of my skull.

I had recently formed my friendship with Azazel, whom I may have mentioned to you.—Oh, I did? Well, all right. You needn't add "ad nauseum" merely to display your knowledge of Latin.

In any case, why shouldn't I use Azazel's abilities in this respect? What was the use of having a two-centimeter extraterrestrial being of advanced technological abilities on call, so to speak, if one didn't make use of it?

I said, "Cousin Andromache, I believe I could train Pussy to show you affection."

"You?" she said, nastily. It was a word, and an intonation, she had used on me before, and I often thought how effectively I would resent it if I were only in a position to do so safely.

But the idea was looking better and better to me as I pictured Cousin Andromache's gratitude to me if I could pull it off.

"Cousin Andromache," I said, earnestly, "let me have Pussy for one day—*one day*. I will then bring back a loving Pussy who will ask for nothing better than to sit in your lap and purr in your ear."

Cousin Andromache hesitated. "Are you sure you will be kind to her while you have her. You know, Pussy is a very sensitive creature, shy and gentle."

Yes, indeed, about as shy and gentle as a particularly irritated grizzly bear.

"I would take very good care of her, Cousin Andromache," I murmured insinuatingly.

And, in the end, Cousin Andromache's longing for an affectionate Pussy overcame her uncertainties and she gave her permission with many an injunction to keep the little thing from being harmed by the cruel, outside world.

Of course, I had to buy a cage first, one with bars as thick as my thumb. This I felt might retain Pussy, if she didn't get too angry, and off we went together.

• • •

Azazel didn't get as angry in those days as he does now when I call him up. He was curious about Earth in those days.

On this occasion, though, what he was, was terrified. He screamed all but ultrasonically. It pierced my eardrums like an icepick.

"What's the matter?" I said, my hands over the affected organs.

"That creature." Azazel's tail pointed to Pussy. "What is it?"

I turned to look at Pussy. It had flattened itself at the bottom of the cage. Its wicked green eyes stared at Azazel with fixed longing. Its tail twitched slowly and then it launched itself at the bars of the cage, which shook and rattled. Azazel screamed again.

"It's just a cat," I said, soothingly. "A little kitten."

"Put me in your pocket," shrieked Azazel. "Put me in your pocket."

On the whole, that seemed a good idea. I plunked him into my shirt-pocket where he trembled like a tuning fork and Pussy, angered and puzzled at his disappearance, spat her displeasure.

Finally, I could make out coherent words from within my pocket.

"Oh, my supple tail," moaned Azazel. "It is just like a drakopathan—just like. They're ferocious beasts that bite and claw and tear, but this cat thing is much bigger and more ferocious by the look of it. Why have you exposed me to this, O Excrescence of a Rubbishy Planet?"

"O Fearless Master of the Universe," I said, "it is precisely in connection with this animal, whose name is Pussy, that I need a demonstration of your matchless might."

"No, no," came his muffled cry.

"It is to make him a better cat. I want Pussy to love my Cousin Andromache who owns the animal. I want Pussy to give my cousin affection and tenderness and sweetness—"

Azazel poked a frightened eye over the top of the pocket and stared at Pussy for a moment. He said, "That creature has no love in it for anything but itself. That is quite obvious from its C-aura."

"Exactly! You must add love for Cousin Andromache."

"What do you mean, add love. Have you never heard of the Law of Conservation of Emotion, you sub-technological dolt. You can't add love. You can only transfer it from one object within a creature's emotional nexus to another."

"Do so," I said. "Take from the superfluity of love Pussy devotes to herself and fashion a strong attachment to Cousin Andromache."

"Taking from the self-love of that super-drakopathan is a task too formidable. I have seen my people strain their intensifiers permanently at lesser tasks."

"Then take the love from elsewhere in Pussy, O Superlative One. Do you wish word to get out that you failed a challenge so small?"

Vanity was, of course, Azazel's besetting fault, and I could see the possibility I had mentioned was gnawing at him.

He said, "Well, I will try. Do you have a likeness of your cousin? A good likeness?"

I certainly had, though I doubt that any photograph of Cousin Andromache could be both a likeness and good at the same time. Putting that philosophical matter to one side, I had a large cabinet photograph of her that I always placed in a prominent position when she came on a visit. I did have to take the fig tree out of the living room on those occasions, though, for the photo had a tendency to wither its leaves.

Azazel looked at the picture dubiously, and sighed. "Very well," he said, "but remember that this is not magic, but science. I can only work within the limits of the Law of Conservation of Emotion."

But what did I care for Azazel's limits of action as long as he did his job?

• • •

The next day I brought Pussy back to Cousin Andromache. Pussy had always been a strong and malevolent cat, but her indifference to others had induced a customary apathy that had kept her evil nature within bounds. Now, apparently, with her sudden wild love for Cousin Andromache frustrated by the absence of her object of affection, she had turned into a demon. She made it quite plain that, were it not for the bars of her cage, which gave dangerously under her pressure, she would tear me into shreds, and I was sure she could do it.

Pussy's mood changed completely, however, when she spied her mistress. The spitting, snarling, slashing devil became at once a panting, purring, picture of delight. She turned on her back, exposing a massively sinewy belly that she clearly wanted scratched.

Cousin Andromache, with a cry of delight, placed a finger through the bars to oblige. I then opened the gate and Pussy went sailing out into Cousin Andromache's waiting arms, purring as loudly as a truck going over a cobbled road, and striving to strop its rasping tongue on my cousin's leathery cheek.

I will draw the curtain over what followed, because it will not bear description. Suffice it to say that, among other things, Cousin Andromache said to the vile cat, "And did you miss your loving Andromache-Womickey?"

It was enough to make me vomicky, let me tell you.

Stolidly, however, I remained, for I was waiting to hear what I wanted to hear and, finally, Cousin Andromache looked up with a pallid glitter in her opaque little eyes and said, "Thank you, Cousin George. I apologize for doubting you, and I promise you I won't forget this to my dying day and will then make you a suitable return."

"It was my pleasure, Cousin Andromache," I said, "and I hope your dying day is far, far in the future."

What was more, if she had at that moment consented to settle a goodly sum on me effective immediately, I believe I would actually have meant what I said.—Within limits.

• • •

I stayed away from Cousin Andromache for a while, not wishing to push my luck, since my presence in her vicinity had, in the past, always seemed to sour her.—I don't know why.

I did phone her every now and then, though, just to make sure all was well, and, to my continuing delight, all *was* well. At least, she would each time trill coyly into my ear, "I love little Pussy", and then cite nauseating details of the cat's affectionate behavior.

x   Then, about three months after I had brought back Pussy, Cousin Andromache called and asked me to drop in for lunch. Naturally, under the circumstances, Cousin Andromache's wish was my law, so I hurried over at the set time. Since she had sounded cheerful on the phone, I had no apprehensions.

Nor did I have any when I entered her apartment, even though I nearly slipped to destruction on the throw-rug she kept on her polished floor near the entrance for what I could only assume were homicidal reasons. She greeted me with what was intended, I imagine, as a jolly grin.

"Come in, Cousin George," she said. "Say hello to little Pussy."

I looked down at little Pussy and shied in horror. Little Pussy, perhaps because it was so full of love, had grown still farther, and at a rapid pace. She seemed nearly three feet along exclusive of lashing tail and I judged her to weigh, conservatively, twenty-five pounds of whipcord and gristle. Her eyes were flat, her mouth was open in a silent snarl, her eye-teeth gleamed like burnished needles, and her eyes, as they glared at me, were filled with indescribable loathing. She stood between Cousin Andromache and me quite as though guarding the silly woman against any false move on my part.

I dared make no move at all, for who knew what that monstrous creature might consider false.

I tried to be strong, but there was a distinct quaver in my

voice as I said, "Is Pussy safe, Cousin Andromache?"

"Perfectly safe," said Cousin Andromache, giggling rather in the same fashion a rusty hinge would, "for she knows you are a relative and mean me well."

"Good," I said, hollowly, wondering if it were possible for Pussy to read my mind. I decided she couldn't or I would not at that moment have been alive, I'm sure.

Cousin Andromache seated herself on the couch and motioned me to take the armchair. However, I waited till Pussy had also jumped on the couch and had placed her head in Cousin Andromache's lap in luxurious abandon, before daring to move sufficiently to sit down myself.

"Of course," said Cousin Andromache, "my loving little Pussy is just a little unreasonable when she thinks someone is trying to harm me. A couple of weeks ago, the newsboy threw the paper just as I was coming out the door. It hit me on the shoulder. It didn't really hurt, but Pussy was after him like a flash. If he hadn't pedalled his bicycle at top speed, I really don't know what would have happened to him. Now the boy won't return and I have to go out every morning and buy the paper at a newsstand. It is comfortable to know, though, that I'm protected from any mugger or burglar."

At the words "mugger or burglar", Little Pussy seemed to be reminded of me, for she turned to look at me and her eyes blazed with the fires of Hell.

It seemed to me I saw what had happened. After all, hate is negative love.

Pussy had had a mild hatred for everything and everyone but herself and, just possibly, Cousin Andromache. To increase Pussy's love for Andromache, Azazel, following the dictates of the Law of Conservation of Emotion, had to withdraw love from all other objects. Since that love was already negative, it grew more negative than ever. And since Azazel had added love with no sparing hand, the other loves grew *much* more negative. In short, Pussy now hated everyone and everything with an extravagant hatred that had strengthened and enlarged her muscles, sharpened her teeth and claws, and turned her into a killing machine.

Cousin Andromache chattered on. "Last week," she said, "Pussy and I were out for a morning stroll and we met Mr. Walsingham with his Doberman-pinscher. I had every intention of avoiding him and crossing the street, but the dog had seen Pussy and snarled at the little innocent creature. Pussy didn't seem to mind, but it frightened me— I don't like dogs at *all*—and I'm afraid I let out a small shriek. That activated dear little Pussy's protective instinct, and she fell on the dog at once. There was no hope of separating them and the dog, I understand, is still at the vet's. Mr. Walsingham is trying to have Pussy declared a dangerous animal, but of course it was the dog that took the initiative and Pussy was merely acting in my defense."

She hugged Pussy as she said that, placing her face in actual contact with the cat's canines, and with no perceptible nervousness. And then she got to the real reason for the invitation to lunch.

She simpered horribly and said, "But I called you here to give you some news I felt I should tell you personally and not on the telephone.—I have a gentleman caller."

"A what!" I jumped slightly, and Pussy at once rose and arched its back. I quickly froze.

I have since thought it out. It seems clear that the sensation of being loved—even if only by a cat out of Golgotha— had softened Cousin Andromache's sinewy heart and made her ready to gaze with eyes of affection on some poor victim. And who knows? Perhaps the consciousness of being loved had changed her inner being to the point of making her seem marginally toothsome to someone particularly dim of vision and particularly lacking in taste.

But that was a later analysis. At the time Cousin Andromache broke the news, my keen mind quickly grasped the vital point—my prosperous relative might possibly have someone else to whom to leave her cash and possessions.

My first impulse was to rise from my seat, seize Cousin

Andromache, and shake some sense of family responsibility into her. My second impulse, following a millisecond later, was not to move a muscle. Pussy's hate-filled eye was on me.

"But Cousin Andromache," I said, "you always told me that if any fellow came lollygagging around you, you'd show *him*! Why not let Pussy show him? That will fix him."

"Oh, no, Hendrik is *such* a nice man and he loves cats, too. He stroked Pussy, and Pussy *let* him. That's when I knew he was all right. Pussy is a good judge of character."

I suppose even Pussy would have trouble matching the look of hatred I let *her* have.

"In any case," said Cousin Andromache, "Hendrik is coming over tonight and I believe he will propose that we formalize conditions by getting married. I wanted you to know."

I tried to say something, but couldn't. I tell you I felt as though I had been thoroughly emptied of my internal organs and I was nothing but hollow skin.

She went on, "I want you also to know, Cousin George, that Hendrik is a retired gentleman, who is quite well off. It is understood between us that, if I predecease him, none of my small savings will go to him. They will go to you, dear Cousin George, as the person who turned Pussy into a loving and efficient companion and protector for me."

Someone had turned the sun and the daylight back on again and all my internal organs were in place once more. It occurred to me, in the merest trice, that if Hendrik predeceased Cousin Andromache, his estate would be very likely added to hers, and would also eventually come to me.

I said, ringingly, "Cousin Andromache. Your money does not concern me. Only your love and your future happiness do. Marry Hendrik, be happy, and live forever. That's all I ask."

I said it with such sincerity, old fellow, that I came within this much of convincing myself I meant it.

• • •

And then, that evening—

I wasn't there, of course, but I found out about it later. Hendrik—seventy, if he was a day, a little over five feet tall and pushing a hundred and eighty pounds in weight— came to call.

She opened the door for him, and skipped skittishly away. He threw his arms wide, called out, "My love!", advanced heavily, slipped on the throw-rug, went hurtling forward into Cousin Andromache feet-first, and bowled her over.

That was all Pussy needed. She knew an attack on her mistress when she saw one. By the time the screaming Andromache pulled the screaming Pussy off screaming Hendrik, it was too late for any hope of a romantic marriage proposal that night. It was indeed very nearly too late for anything at all that would involve Hendrik.

Two days later, I visited him at the hospital at Cousin Andromache's hysterical request. He was still bandaged to the eyebrows and a team of doctors were discussing the various possible strategies of skin-grafting.

I introduced myself to Hendrik, who wept copiously, drenching his bandages, and begged me to tell my fair relative that all this was a visitation upon him for being unfaithful to his first wife, Emmeline, dead these seventeen years, and for even dreaming of marrying anyone at all.

"Tell her," he said, "we will always be the dearest of friends, but I dare not ever see her again, for I am but flesh and blood and the sight of her might arouse loving thoughts and I would then once more be attacked by a grizzly bear."

I carried the sad news to Cousin Andromache, who took to her bed at once, crying out that through her doing, the best of men had been permanently maimed—which was undoubtedly true.

The rest, old man, is unalloyed tragedy. I would have sworn that Cousin Andromache was incapable of dying of a broken heart, but a team of specialists maintained that that was exactly what she proceeded to do. That was sad, I suppose, but the unalloyed tragedy I refer to was that she had had time to alter her will.

In the new will, she expressed her great affection for me and her certainty that I was far too noble to concern myself over a few pennies so that she left her entire estate of $300,000 not to me, but to her lost love, Hendrik, hoping it would make up to him for the suffering and the medical bills he had incurred because of her.

All this was expressed in terms so affecting that the lawyer who read the will to me wept uncontrollably and so, as you can well imagine, did I.

However, I was not entirely forgotten. Cousin Andromache stated in her will that she left me something she knew I would value far more than the paltry dross of cash. In short she had left me Pussy.

George just sat there, staring numbly at nothingness and I couldn't help saying, "Do you still have Pussy?"

He started, focussed on me with an effort, and said, "No, not exactly. The very day I received her, she was trampled by a horse."

"By a horse!"

"Yes. The horse died of its wounds the next day. A shame, for it was an innocent horse. It's fortunate, on the whole, that no one had seen me open Pussy's cage and shake her into the horse's stall."

His eyes glazed over again, and his lips mouthed, silently: Three—hundred—thousand—dollars!

Then he turned to me and said, "So can you lend me a tenner?"

What could I do?

JAMES MORROW

ONLY BEGOTTEN DAUGHTER

"...RAUCOUSLY SATISFYING."—<u>The New York Times</u>

A baby daughter was born to the virgin Murray Katz, and her name is Julie. Call it a miracle. Call it the Second Coming. Call it a mishap at the sperm bank. One thing is for sure—this could only happen in New Jersey. Julie can heal the blind, raise the dead, and generate lots of publicity. In fact, the poor girl needs a break, even if it means a vacation in Hell (which is unseasonably warm). So what did you expect? It ain't easy being the Daughter of God...

___ONLY BEGOTTEN DAUGHTER 0-441-63041-3/$4.50

THIS IS THE WAY THE WORLD ENDS

"The only book in the last ten years that I have read twice...a remarkable achievement."—Arthur C. Clarke

George Paxton was an ordinary man, living an ordinary life. Until something extraordinary happened. Something that the United States and the Soviet Union had been spending a large amount of diligence and money to bring about. Some called it a nuclear holocaust. Others said it was the end of the world. Now, George Paxton is about to discover what happens after the end of the world...

___THIS IS THE WAY THE WORLD ENDS 0-441-80711-9/$3.95